To Priscilla ... It

I heard you couldn't ... for this copy... thanks for the Love.. Teen

Empty Pleasures

Empty Pleasures

Once a good girl goes bad is she really gone forever?

Icen

Higher Realm Publishing

EMPTY PLEASURES

Published by Higher Realm Publishing
P.O. Box 710102
Oak Hill, VA 20171

This book is a work of fiction. The characters, incidents, and dialogue are drawn from the author's imagination and are not to be construed as real. Any resemblance to actual events or persons, living or dead, is entirely coincidental.

FIRST EDITION

Icen is a trademark registered in the U.S. Patent and Trademark Office.

Printed in the United States of America

ISBN 978-0-615-28716-4

Library of Congress Control Number: 2009925168

Edited by James Keith
Designed by Jessica Tilles
Poems by Joyce Newsome Bates

In loving memory of my sister,

Traci Rochelle Bates

1970—2008

Acknowledgements

All praises to God!—Sovereign giver of life. Nothing moves or exists without Him. I bless your Holy name for showing me daily just how much You love me.

Darryl and Deven, my brilliant sons, thank you for being patient and sharing me with my dream to write a novel. You have both been a tremendous part of this journey; especially in helping with certain details I probably drove you crazy about. But the book is finished for real this time. I love you! To my mom, thanks for listening to me babble on about finishing the book and for allowing me to use your poems. I consider it a perfect gift from God that He chose me to come through you into this world. God bless you! Tommy, big bro, thanks for calming me down about the corrupt disk files. Your patience was just what I needed. Shout out to Gilda, Tommy III and Khory. To the Bates family in Birmingham, AL, thanks for loving me through a very sad time in my life. I'll always remember the daily text messages and concern you showed me. To my spiritual advisors—you know who you are—thanks for giving me what God gave you. Carolyn, I hope you can add this one to your list of favorites. Sheena...mission accomplished! See you on the big screen, Sheena Emgee! Ellen, Michael T. and Julie, thanks for your encouraging words—you give me momentum. James Keith your critiques and suggestions were on the money. Jessica Tilles, author and publisher extraordinaire, thanks for your invaluable advice and for the book and cover design. To Gary Johnson, Founder and Publisher of BlackMenInAmerica.com, thanks for publishing my very first article over a year ago, and all the opportunities you threw my way. I finally reached my goal!

To the reader, I pray this story will make you laugh, think, cry, and realize the healing, transforming power of true love.

Peace,
Icen

Singles and Sex

What is singles and sex? Singles and sex
is giving a little of your soul to this one
and that one; and receiving a little of this
one and that one's soul, until you are unsure
of who you are and what you believe.

Singles and sex causes you to ask the
question, who is the lord of my life?

I tell you what, ask the Lord Jesus Christ
to become Lord of your life and bring your
scattered soul back in oneness with you.

Chapter 1

"Whose is it?" Marvin asked. Sweat dripping from every inch of his body.

I hate when he says that dumb shit, Bobbi thought.

"Turn over baby." He flipped Bobbi over on her stomach and pulled her up onto her knees. He moaned. "Yeah, just like that." His eyes closed and his head fell backwards as he pulled her into him repeatedly. "You like that, don't you?"

Bobbi didn't answer. The quiver he felt in her body was not from pleasure but from the silent sobs she held back. All she wanted was for him to be finished.

Each stroke came harder, faster. Everything moved to his cadence—her hair, her body, the squeaky bed and the wooden headboard slamming against the wall. Bobbi felt like a rag doll. She tried to grab hold of his slippery black satin sheets to steady herself but it didn't help.

Marvin growled as he got closer to his climax. He gripped her hips tighter—his muscles stiffened. He grunted. Seconds later he collapsed on her back.

"Get off me," Bobbi gritted through clinched teeth. His sweaty skin against her smooth dry back disgusted her. She struggled to pull herself from under his weight. “I said get up, Marvin. I need to use the bathroom.”

His breathing still irregular, he rolled off of her onto his back. Before she was able to get her footing, he smacked her ass so hard it seemed to echo off the bare walls of his bedroom.

“Ouch!” She rubbed her cheek to lighten the sting. “I told you I don’t like it when you do that.”

Marvin opened his eyes and grinned. He raised his head off the bed and reached for one of her legs but she moved away. “Girl, stop playin’,” he replied. “You know you like that.” When he realized she was serious, he fell back on the bed and closed his eyes.

Bobbi mumbled expletives under her breath and gestured her hands as if choking his neck. She was tempted to actually do it but knew she couldn’t pull it off so she stumped off naked across the stained tan carpet to his master bathroom.

Locking the door behind her, she stared in the mirror. Her shoulder length black hair was tousled and mascara was smeared underneath her bottom lashes. But it was the sadness in the green eyes that stared back at her that held her attention. Why had she just let Marvin sex her without protection? A sick feeling settled in the pit of her stomach.

After nearly two years of lies, Marvin’s trifling ways had finally caught up to him. Before now, whenever she heard something about him being with other women she would blow it off—chalking it up as rumors from the many haters who wanted to break them up. But a few days ago she had received a sobering dose of truth about her man through a telephone call she couldn’t get out of her head.

You don't know me, but my name is Janae. Marvin was in my bed last night when you were blowing up his cell. The next time you're looking for him, just call me. You have the number now.

Warm tears trickled down her honey-brown cheeks. How could Marvin cheat on her and act like nothing happened? Three nights ago they were supposed to spend a quiet evening together to try and rekindle that burning flame they used to have for one another. Or at least those were Bobbi's intentions. But Marvin didn't show up or even call to say he wasn't coming; and he didn't bother answering any of her calls. She must have called him twenty times. Finally he called the next day with some ridiculous excuse about one of his boys needing a ride somewhere because his car wasn't working.

Marvin jiggled the door knob and knocked. "What's taking you so long, boo? I gotta pee."

Bobbi rolled her eyes. "Hold up. I'll be out in a minute," she shouted, snatching tissues from the box on the sink.

Moments later Marvin knocked again. "Come on, B. Open the damn door, girl!"

Bobbi snapped. "Wait!" She finished cleaning herself up, combed her hair into a ponytail and unlocked the door.

As soon as Marvin heard the click of the lock, he pushed the door open knocking Bobbi into the sink as he rushed past her to relieve himself.

"What's your problem?" he asked, holding his manhood. "What took you so long to open the door?" Although he asked the question, he already knew what her problem was—him. He hadn't said anything to her about standing her up the other night, and neither had she. And he hoped things stayed that way because there was no way on earth he could tell her the truth—that he had flaked on her to get some of that big booty Janae had been teasing him with.

Bobbi's eyes traveled the length of his naked six-feet-two muscular physique then settled on the very body part that had betrayed her. "My only problem is you," she scowled.

He didn't say a word—just finished his business and flushed the toilet. Bobbi looked at him and shook her head. So predictable, she thought. Whenever he messed up, he either lied or got quiet. So he was playing it safe by keeping his big lips closed. He didn't want any skeletons to come tumbling out of his mouth.

Bobbi grabbed her comb from the sink, which had been in his medicine cabinet for forever, and went back into his room without saying another word. He closed the door behind her.

She paced the floor trying to clear her head but it wasn't working. She wanted Marvin to pay for hurting her—for taking advantage of her love and making her feel foolish. But she had to be crafty because there was no way she could fight his big behind if things got out of control.

Still wondering how she could get even, Bobbi picked her clothes up off the floor and got dressed. The sound of the shower was like music to her ears. This was her opportunity to get out of there without a confrontation. As much as she loved Marvin, she was too upset with him to care about anything he possibly had to say about the Janae situation. This relationship was over.

So she gathered the few things she had tucked away in the one drawer he said was hers. T-shirts, a pair of sweat pants, underwear and a bottle of Mango scented body lotion—basically loungewear for when she stayed overnight. Ten minutes had passed since she heard the shower turn on so there wasn't much time left to do what she was thinking.

Quickly, she opened his closet and ripped clothes off the hangers, throwing some on the closet floor while tossing others in the room on the floor. Next she turned over his shoe boxes and pulled his treasured baseball caps off the shelf. Then she walked over to the bed and pulled off what was left of the covers and pushed over the top mattress. At his dresser, in one sweep of each drawer, she whisked his underwear, t-shirts and socks all over the floor. And for the heck of it, she threw a pair of boxer briefs and a couple of socks on the ceiling fan blades. By the time she finished, it looked like the police had raided his bedroom looking for drugs.

Bobbi dusted her hands together and nodded her approval—pleased with her handiwork. Surely Marvin should have been out of the bathroom by now, but he was probably staying in there to avoid the onslaught of questions and drama he thought she would bring to him.

Ready to go, Bobbi grabbed her bag and keys. Just then the shower finally turned off. Marvin was going to flip out when he saw his room, she thought. But if he knew like she did, he would count his blessings that she took her anger out on his clothes and not his nuts like she wanted to.

In less time than it would take to step out of the shower, grab a towel and dry off, Bobbi was out of his apartment.

The coolness of the mid-November night air made her pull her coat together. But it didn't stop her from moving quickly down two flights of stairs to the parking lot. She opened the door of her red two-door Honda Civic, threw her bag of clothes in the back seat and jumped in to get as far away as she could from 1214 Sycamore Lane, Apt. 303B.

Chapter 2

Bobbi and Marvin were both in the military stationed in the Washington, DC area. When they met through a mutual friend two years ago, Bobbi was only twenty-years-old—four years his junior. For her it was love at first sight. Born and raised in Atlanta, she wasn't accustomed to the swagger and smooth talk of a New Yorker. And he definitely had his hometown swag working. But his smooth confident demeanor and hip hop style weren't the only reasons she was weak for him. The way he attended to her needs, always asking if she was okay, and the affection he showed her in the beginning made her feel so special. And sexually he was a beast. He did things to her young inexperienced body that no man had. Every woman on base wanted a piece of her cocoa brown stallion. She was on top of the world when they were together.

Bobbi did whatever he wanted her to do and gave whatever she thought would keep him interested, demanding very little in return. She was a firm believer in what she'd heard other woman say: a woman had to keep her man satisfied or he would stray. And that's the last thing she wanted to happen. Sharing her man was out of the question.

Yet, to her dismay, after the first year of their relationship, she began to sense that he was loosing interest in her. It didn't seem to matter to him whether they spent quality time together or not. He was always busy on Friday nights which had been their date night since day one. Entire weekends would go by without her seeing him. Lately, she felt like all she was to him was a booty call. And he seemed perfectly fine with things the way they were. Whenever she tried to talk to him about their relationship he would say, "You know I love you, ma, so why you trippin'? It's all good."

But now it didn't matter what he said. That call from Janae had been a very painful wake-up call—one she would be a fool to ignore. And she was nobody's fool. So it was time to count her losses and move on with her life.

On the ride home from Marvin's house, fresh tears fell. Not so much for her failed relationship with Marvin because she had been loosing that battle for some time now. But her tears fell because she felt confused and rejected. It just didn't seem that she was enough for any man she'd ever loved.

Thankfully she was approaching a red light because she could hardly see through the pooled tears in her eyes. Bobbi reached over and opened the glove compartment looking for fast food napkins she usually threw in there. Just then her cell phone rang. *Ugh*! Marvin's name was on the caller-id.

Bobbi rolled her eyes upward. As much as she didn't want to talk to him, she was expecting his call. Threw her tears, a mischievous grin reached her lips imaging his reaction to his precious hip hop gear and underwear strewn all over his bedroom floor.

"Hello." Bobbi answered curtly.

"Yo, B? Why you tear up my damn room like this?" Marvin was mad. A hand on his waist, he looked at his things scattered about the floor.

The light changed so Bobbi put him on speaker. "Ask Janae, stupid ass," she mumbled driving off. "You know, all this time I believed you when you said you weren't cheating on me. You always denied everything. Humph. But you can't lie this time." Bobbi was furious. "And just so you know, I'm done–"

"Whoa, whoa. Wait a minute." He cut her off. "Janae called you?" Marvin pushed his mattress back on the bed and sat down. That comment threw him for a loop. He figured Bobbi was still salty with him about not showing up and not answering his phone the other night, but he didn't know Janae had called her.

Click. Without another word Bobbi flipped her phone shut. She could spit fire right about now. Not only had he cheated on her, but his dumb ass had just admitted to it by his reaction to hearing that Janae had called her.

I know she didn't just hang up on me. Marvin looked at his phone in disbelief. He had to admit though, what he did was messed up. In all the time he'd been with Bobbi, he had never left her hanging like he did Tuesday night. But he couldn't help it. Janae had a fat ass and she wouldn't leave him alone. A man could only have so much self control. Right now Bobbi was too upset to listen to him so he would give her space and time to cool off. But he hoped it wouldn't take her too long to get over this little episode because she was his "ol' faithful" as he liked to think of her.

He was a single man with a hearty sexual appetite and liked to try something strange and different when the mood hit him.

But he had molded Bobbi into his little sex genie. Every freaky fantasy he was able to dream up was only a wish away. *Damn.* He got up and paced the floor; realization had kicked in. He couldn't lose Bobbi no matter what. Not for all the other chicken heads he dealt with, including Janae.

Bobbi's emotions were all over the place. One minute she couldn't stop the tears from flowing, and the next minute she felt like a fire breathing dragon. She needed to talk. So she pressed the number three button on her cell phone to speed dial her best friend and confidante, Nikki.

"What's up girly? What's good?" a bubbly Nikki asked. Bobbi often referred to her as the Energizer Bunny.

"Nothing," she replied dryly. "I'm on my way home from dog nuts house."

Nikki laughed. "Dog nuts? You're crazy, girl. So what's up with that fool tonight anyway?" she asked still laughing.

"It's over. That's what's up."

"You're kidding me?"

"Nope. And I mean it. So please, if you ever hear me say anything remotely related to being with him again, you have my permission to chop off one of my boobs."

Nikki's mouth fell open. "Dang, girl." She chuckled. "Do I need to get you some help? I mean that's some *Hannibal Lector* type shit you just said." Bobbi had to be past upset because she didn't usually say crazy stuff like that. Nikki was the one with the over-the-top commentary and slick one-liners. "Well, I don't think I can chop your boob off, but I get your point." She laughed out loud.

Bobbi was too serious to see the humor. "Good. Can we meet for lunch tomorrow? I really need to talk."

"Yeah, that's cool. I'll be out early shopping anyway." As if singing, she continued, "*Macy's* is calling me...ca-ca-calling me." Nikki was a shop-a-holic. It was all about the glitz, glamour and fabulosity with her. "You want to come?"

"Uh-uh. I don't feel like fighting the crowds. Just let me know when you're ready for a break and I'll meet you somewhere close to the mall.

"Okay. Talk to you tomorrow. Peace."

From baby dolls to dating to now—out on their own finding their way in life, Bobbi and Nikki were more like sisters than best friends. Bobbi's mom, Grace, and Nikki's mom, Tina, were childhood friends who remained close throughout school. However, to their dismay they grew apart when they went away to different colleges. But as fate would have it, when Bobbi was ten, she and her mom unknowingly moved into the house across the street from Nikki's family. When Tina and Nikki went over to welcome their new neighbors to the neighborhood, both Grace and Tina got the biggest surprise of their lives. The old friends embraced and talked none stop for days. They had nearly fifteen years to catch up on.

Bobbi and Nikki were introduced to each other as God sisters and hit it off instantly. Their mothers vowed to raise them like sisters—like family. Now Bobbi and Nikki were carrying on a generational sisterhood.

Nevertheless, unique in their own personality, style, and life goals, after high school Bobbi and Nikki chose different paths.

Nikki always dreamed of being an attorney after watching the character Terri on the series *Soul Food*. Now she was a student at *Howard University* preparing to graduate in six months.

For Bobbi, school was the farthest thing on her mind after graduation—or so she thought. So she enlisted in the military. But she and Nikki never lost contact. Actually, Bobbi had managed to spend her entire four-year enlistment in the Washington, DC, area which left the two only minutes apart. So they continued to relish a true comfort of home—their close friendship.

Chapter 3

Bobbi fell across her twin sized bed with a heavy sigh. It was one A.M. and she couldn't sleep. She looked around her efficiency sized dorm room. On the far wall across from her bed was a chocolate brown futon with red and lime green decorative pillows which matched the ones on her bed. Cat-a-corner from the futon was a cherry wood pub style table with two matching bar stools. Other than the thirty-seven inch television mounted in the ceiling near her bed and a small table next to her bed, there wasn't much else to see. But she loved her small colorful space. Whenever she came home from a hard day at work or felt down about anything, the vibrant splashes of color would brighten her mood. However, tonight her melancholy disposition wouldn't allow it.

Just when she'd found some semblance of peace after all the drama earlier tonight, Marvin started blowing up her cell. Although she didn't answer, she listened to the selfish, arrogant voice messages he left. He said that he forgave her for tearing up his room, and that she was insecure for believing what another woman told her about him. He even had the audacity to say that if she wanted their relationship to work, she had to stop being so jealous.

He had some nerve. It ticked her off when Marvin talked to her like she should be honored to be with him. She was no slouch. Popular opinion among the men on base was that Bobbi ranked number one in the fine-ass-woman, top-shelf category. Her body had curves in all the right places—her measurements 36-26-36. Even in uniform with her thick black hair pinned up, the five-feet-six beauty turned heads.

But her looks didn't scratch the surface of who she really was. She was intelligent with a great personality and big dreams. For example, along with fulfilling her military commitment, she was working towards a degree in Communications in the evenings after work and had plans to open her own PR Firm one day. And she was well on her way to making that dream a reality after her discharge from active duty in eight months. From there, if she worked really hard, in one year she would have her degree. And Marvin knew this about her. That's why she couldn't understand why he treated her like some naïve, desperate hooker at times.

She rolled over and stared at the ceiling. Her mom and Aunt Tina always told her and Nikki that they should keep relationships on the lighter side while in their twenties. That they shouldn't expect for every guy they meet to be "the one." But Bobbi didn't see what was so wrong with that.

Restless, she shifted back to her stomach and reached for a pillow. She tucked the pillow under her chin and picked up the remote to mute the television. Exhaling deeply, she wondered what she was doing wrong.

Why does it seem like I'm good enough for sex but never good enough for a man to be loyal to me? I consider myself a "good girl" as men say (whatever that means). I only date one guy at a time. And I only sleep with one man at a time—except for that one summer, but that's beside the point. The point is I limit what I do and who I do it with. I mean...is it too much to expect Marvin, or any other man for that matter, to only want to be with me?

Bobbi cried herself to sleep.

Saturday morning, Nikki called Bobbi on her way to the mall. She knew it was too early for Bobbi to be up moving around but she just couldn't help herself.

"Hey, chick-a-dee. You up?" came Nikki's lively voice.

"What time is it? Bobbi asked, still drowsy.

"Six o'clock."

Bobbi checked her watch on the table next to her bed. She smacked her lips.

"Girl, why are you calling me so early? You better have a good reason for waking me up."

"No. I just wanted to say good morning. Good morning!" Nikki snickered.

"Bye!" Bobbi hung up the phone, turned over and pulled the covers over her head. Hopefully she could fall back asleep for at lest three more hours.

Around ten o'clock, Nikki called back and they made plans to meet at Claude's, a popular sports bar near the Spring Valley Mall. After Bobbi showered and dressed in boot-cut blue jeans, a camel colored turtleneck sweater and her favorite brown wedged heeled shoes she pulled her hair into a ponytail, grabbed her brown leather jacket and headed out the door.

The sky was gray but the temperature was sixty degrees; a stark contrast to the chilly air last night. It looked like it would rain at any moment. Bobbi pulled at her turtle neck and started up the car. R&B blared from the car speakers. She loved all types of music but Rhythm & Blues was her favorite because it connected with her emotions. However, today she wasn't in the mood for love songs. She wanted to throw up when the singer on the radio crooned on about his special lover. *Yuck!*

Bobbi pulled out her CD case and popped in some *Mary J Blige*. She selected the track she now deemed her theme song: *No More Drama*. By the time she pulled into the restaurant parking lot, she had listened to it five times, singing at the top of her lungs.

As expected, there was no sign of Nikki. Bobbi smiled knowing that Nikki was probably up in *Macy's* in a trance. So she drove around the lot looking for two available spaces close together and parked. She turned the car off and pumped *Mary* even louder while she waited.

Within fifteen minutes Nikki came barreling into the parking lot and rolled her twin candy red Civic into the space next to Bobbi. She had a smile on her face a mile wide. Both their cars were graduation presents from their parents. The only difference in the two cars was their license plates. Bobbi's read: B OUT; while Nikki's read: N WHAT.

They got out of their cars and brushed air kisses to each others cheeks.

"Uh, didn't we say two o'clock? What took you so long?" Bobbi asked.

"Girl, don't even ask." Nikki tugged at Bobbi's arm. "Wait till you see what I picked up this morning. You know *Macy's* had that early bird special, right?" She swallowed hard and continued. "Well, that was in addition to the all day shopping pass. You're gonna die when you see the boots I got. Ooh, girl. I got so dizzy and excited up in there I almost forgot we were meeting for lunch." She fanned herself.

Bobbi shook her head and used the back of her hand to check Nikki's forehead for fever. "Something is seriously wrong with you. Nobody gets that worked up over a sale."

A group of guys walking towards a car a few feet away whistled at them. But this was nothing new. The two stopped traffic every where they went. Nikki was a tad shorter than Bobbi—her skin the color of honey. She had curves in all the right places too, but slightly more petite.

Nikki turned to see who was whistling at them. Bobbi didn't.

"Anyway." Bobbi said ignoring them. "I'll check your boots out after we eat. Let's go inside." She looked up at the clouds and started walking. "I think it's going to rain."

Inside, they waited in a short line to be seated.

"How many in your party?" asked the petite red head hostess. "Smoking or nonsmoking?"

"Two," Bobbi replied. "Nonsmoking."

The hostess nodded and showed them to a booth near the bar.

"Your server will be with you shortly."

"Thank you," they both said with half smiles.

Nikki turned her attention to Bobbi. "So what's up? I know you've been down lately about Marvin, but when you called me last night you seemed different. What happened between you two to make you finally decide to leave him alone?"

Bobbi fiddled with the corners of napkin. "I'm just tired of feeling used, you know? You give a man everything you've got and it's still not enough." She almost didn't feel like rehashing the story. But that's why they were there so she went on. She told Nikki about the dinner plans Marvin skipped out on, and the call she received from Janae. When she told her about ransacking his bedroom, Nikki fell out laughing.

A blond boyish looking waitress with an earring in the corner of her mouth and right eyebrow interrupted.

"Hello, my name is Amy. I'll be your server. Can I get you something to drink?"

"Yes," they both said. Bobbi ordered a Piña Colada and a glass of water with lemon. And Nikki ordered a Strawberry Daiquiri with whip cream on top.

"Are you ladies ready to order?"

"Give us a minute." Nikki responded. Bobbi was deep in thought.

Nikki looked at Bobbi for her to continue.

Bobbi sighed heavily. Her shoulders slumped forward. "You know, I've been ride-or-die in every relationship I've been in—even the ones I constructed in my own mind. But I think I'm done with trying to make a man love me. It's just too much to deal with finding out someone you've devoted yourself to could walk all over your emotions like it's nothing."

"Ease up, B." Nikki didn't like the tone of Bobbi's voice or the defeated attitude she saw in her friend. "Marvin and no other man are worth you changing who you are. Fuck Marvin," she blurted. "You just need to make better choices from the jump. I told you his ass was too fine when I met him. But I know you like the cocky, edgy type." Nikki shook her head. "All that swagger ain't worth the trouble."

Amy returned with their drinks and stood waiting to scribble their orders on her pad. Bobbi ordered the grilled shrimp linguine with Alfredo sauce, and Nikki selected the pan seared Tilapia and steamed vegetables.

The two continued to talk through lunch—Nikki doing more listening than talking. She realized Bobbi needed to unload—to get it all out.

Nikki wanted to shout, Hallelujah! It was high time her best friend dumped Marvin. She couldn't stomach being around him with his self serving attitude, but occasionally she did for Bobbi's sake. Nikki point blank didn't like him; however, she never tried to influence Bobbi one way or the other. She just trusted that with time his dirt would come to the light. Karma was a bitch.

The rain was coming down pretty heavy by the time Bobbi and Nikki finished their meals. So they decided to splurge on calories and have dessert while they waited for the rain to slack up.

Nikki got Amy's attention while she was tending to patrons at another table and asked for dessert menus. When she brought them back, Nikki and Bobbi flipped through the plastic covered pages trying to decide what to get.

"What about the Key Lime pie?" Bobbi asked Nikki.

Nikki turned up her nose. "I wanted something chocolate." She kept flipping through the same four pages undecided.

"May I suggest something," Amy interrupted. "Our Chocolate Quake is quite popular. It has two brownies topped with Vanilla ice cream, sprinkled with pecans, and drenched in hot caramel and fudge topping. It's really good."

"Umm, that sounds delicious." Nikki looked at Bobbi for her response.

"Yeah, let's get that. We can share it." Bobbi said.

Amy made a note and took their menus. She cleared their empty plates from the table and left. When she returned with the Chocolate Quake, both Bobbi and Nikki's mouths watered. Good thing they planned to share because it was way too much for an individual serving.

Bobbi shoved a spoon full of the confection in her mouth.

"I think I'm going to take a break from men for awhile," she said before filling her spoon again. "You know, figure out what I want. I have some big things coming up with my discharged from the Air Force, and finishing school so I really don't have time for any more distractions."

Nikki licked the back of her spoon. "That may not be a bad idea," she said pointing her spoon towards Bobbi. "You know, you're damaged goods right now. There's no way you could have a healthy relationship or even a healthy conversation with a man at this point," Nikki teased. "All you would do is fuck up the next mofo's head for women like me who already know what we want—dem dollar-dollar-bills y'all. You heard?"

For the first time in a while, Bobbi laughed. Talking to Nikki had been just what she needed to help her work through her feelings. A glance out the window revealed the sun peeking through the clouds. The rain had passed over. Just like Marvin, Bobbi thought. She smiled. Although she was hurt and uncertain about any future involvement with men, one thing she knew for certain: her blinded by love days were history.

Chapter 4

Five Years Later

Baltimore International Airport was buzzing with early-bird travelers. Mixed in the crowd was Bobbi, on her way to Atlanta to hopefully seal the deal with her first NFL prospect. If everything went according to plan, Atlanta Condor's star quarterback, Terry Barnes, would be signing on as a full service client with her PR Firm, My Way Communications.

After clearing through security, which she absolutely hated doing this morning, she stopped at a café on the concourse for her departure gate to get a French Vanilla cappuccino. While in line she noticed a man stirring his coffee at the condiments bar looking in her direction. He caught her eye because he was quite attractive—cinnamon brown completion, well groomed—a well put together brother. *Definitely fine*, she thought. *Humph*. Bobbi turned her attention back to her place in line and moved forward to place her order.

"Good morning. Can I help you," asked the chipped tooth older woman behind the counter.

"Yes. I'll have a French Vanilla cappuccino."

"One French Vanilla cappuccino," the cashier announced to the staff making the coffee orders.

"That'll be three ninety five." The cashier looked at Bobbi.

Bobbi swiped her card, signed the electronic pad and took her receipt. Then she stepped aside to wait for her order.

She checked her watch. It was only five forty-five. The volume of people moving through the terminal was amazing. Why did so many people like traveling this early? If not for her early business meeting, Bobbi would still be tucked away in her king sized bed counting the cracks in her eyelids.

After all the nonsense she went through with airport security this morning, she may reconsider scheduling out-of-town meetings before noon. First she took off her shoes and put them in the same bin as her laptop, but security wanted her laptop in a separate bin. Then they told her she needed separate bins for her purse and her jacket. Once she finally obeyed all of those orders, they pulled her aside saying that she had been randomly selected for a more thorough search. For the love of God! It was just too early for all of that.

"French Vanilla cappuccino," yelled a deep male voice behind the counter.

"That's me." Bobbie stepped forward and took her cup. "Uh, it's pretty hot. Do you have a sleeve for the cup?" She held the cup with one hand covering the lid, and the other underneath the bottom of the cup.

"Yeah, over there." He pointed to the condiments bar.

Why in heck don't they have some behind the counter, she thought. "Thank you." She got the sleeve and some napkins, took a sip of her cappuccino and headed for Gate 5.

She found a seat near an electrical outlet so she could power up her laptop. One last look at her presentation and her notes wouldn't hurt. Based on the departure monitors she passed on the way to the gate, her flight was scheduled to leave on time. So she had roughly thirty minutes to wait before boarding started.

The internet had been Bobbi's main source for information about Terry. But she had also asked around the athlete circuit through her personal connections for information. Knowing as much as possible about a client was something she took very seriously. It's what gave her an edge in her line of business.

She took a sip of her cappuccino and glanced around the seating area. This was a very important meeting for her firm. Terry's agent mentioned that he had been contacted by some other PR firms already. But that didn't bother Bobbi. She only hoped that he was keeping an open mind until he heard from her today because she had every intention on leaving Atlanta with his signature on a contract.

Bobbi yawned. Getting up at oh-dark-thirty was beginning to come down on her. So she shut down her laptop, deciding to people-watch until boarding. That's when she noticed the attractive gentleman from the café sitting in a row of chairs facing her on the other side of the check-in counter.

Is he looking at me? Bobbi turned around to see if there was someone behind her that he may have been focused on. But the back of other waiting passengers' heads was all she saw. When she turned back around his eyes were still on her.

Maybe she knew him from somewhere—perhaps a business or social event, she thought. But she couldn't place him. Then she thought that maybe he recognized her from somewhere. Either way, his stare was making her uncomfortable. She felt her forehead sizzle from the hole he was burning in it.

Unable to make any sense out of it, Bobbi shrugged it off. She drank the last of her coffee, gathered her purse and carry-on with wheels, and went to stand near the gate ramp.

Chapter 5

As the plane ascended Bobbi rested her head against the headrest, closed her eyes and said a prayer. It never hurt to ask God's blessings upon the plane and pilot. Besides, she had a lot to be thankful for and looked forward to her return flight home. Things were going extremely well in her life, especially in business. Her pending meeting with Terry Barnes was just another example of how blessed she was.

Only four years in business, Bobbi had managed to position My Way Communications as a leading urban entertainment PR Firm in the Washington, DC, area. Six strategically selected clients had yielded huge returns. And signing a major athlete would take her business to the next level. Referrals had been the key to her fast-track success. So making sure Terry was taken care of meant he would send his friends and associates her way. Life was good.

In Atlanta, she deplaned and followed the signs to ground transportation. The anonymous man from the café and his companion were just ahead of her. Who was this guy? Something about him made Bobbi want to know. But she wasn't so pressed that she would make the first move.

She frowned. Why was she putting unnecessary energy into thinking about this stranger? She had a much bigger fish to fry, namely Terry Barnes. Eyeing the Restroom sign ahead to her right, she took a detour to freshen up for her meeting. The couple from the plane disappeared down an escalator.

After washing her hands, she checked herself in the full length mirror. She looked amazing. Her make-up was flawless. Mascara, eyeliner, neutral eye shadow and perfectly arched brows, framed her eyes. Sleek black hair hung to the middle of her back, compliments of the best quality weave she could afford. Usually she wore her hair with a side part and loose body curls, but lately she had it styled bone straight with Chinese bangs.

The knee length skirt of the tailor-made white suit she wore fit nicely on her small waist and hugged the curve of her shapely backside. She wore a black sleeveless drop neck sheath underneath the single button jacket that fastened slightly above her waist. Black four inch stilettos topped off her look.

Her accessories were all set in platinum. She wore classic round diamond stud earrings, a Gucci watch on one wrist, and a link bracelet on the other. One simple diamond ring adorned each hand. She was polished. Before she left, she applied peach frosted gloss to her full lips and rubbed them together. With a wink of approval she said aloud, "Go get'em tiger!"

Exiting the terminal, the humid June air hit Bobbi's lungs like a ton of bricks. She gasped. The sweltering heat and humidity of the south was no joke. If there was a "hell" reading on the thermometer, that's where the mercury would stay from June to September.

Bobbi fanned herself as she stepped off the curb to look for the driver Terry Barnes' agent, Jim Kendall, had sent for her. She reached in her purse for tissues to dab at the moisture forming on her forehead. Just then she saw a middle-aged man in a black suit with big eyes, a big mustache and stained teeth holding up a sign bearing her name. His skin was the color of sun brewed tea.

Bobbi waved her hand. "I'm Bobbi Farqua," she said, approaching the driver.

"Hello Miss Farqua. I'm Eugene your driver," he greeted her in a deep southern drawl. "The car is over here." He pointed a few feet away.

"It's a pleasure to meet you, Eugene."

He nodded and reached for her bag which contained her laptop and important papers. Bobbi followed him to the black Lincoln Towne car with dark tinted windows. He opened the passenger-side back door for her and she climbed inside.

"Ahhh. That's more like it," she breathed, thankful for the assault of cool air blowing from the vents.

Eugene walked around the car to lay her bag on the seat next to her before letting himself in.

"We should arrive at the Lakeview Professional Building in about thirty minutes. Rush hour is almost over so it shouldn't take longer than that. May I ask what time is your meeting?"

"My meeting's at ten thirty."

Eugene nodded. "Yes, ma'am," he said as he pulled into airport traffic.

Jim's offer to send a driver had been just what Bobbi needed. It allowed her to focus completely on her impending meeting and not the crazy Atlanta rush-hour traffic. She leaned back into the soft leather seat, and closed her eyes.

"How was your flight, Miss Farqua?" Eugene blurted, breaking her train of thought.

Bobbi opened her eyes. "We left DC on time, which was a small miracle in itself. And we landed on time. So I would say the flight was excellent." Her tone was pleasant and upbeat.

She turned to look out the dark tinted window. The sky was powder blue without a cloud in it; the sun only halfway to its highest point. It was a beautiful day. She smiled. For some reason she felt really good about this meeting. The anticipation made her tingle all over.

She reached in her purse for her make-up bag and pulled out a mirror. Thank goodness her make-up hadn't melted and her hair was still in place. The humidity in Atlanta could turn straight hair into afro puffs in a snap. She dusted her face with a little loose powder and touched up her lip gloss. Feeling a bit full of herself she thought: *If a big butt and a smile was all a man needed to loss his mind, Terry Barnes would be a drooling, speechless nut case once he laid eyes on her.*

Chapter 6

Fairview Towers was located in the heart of downtown Atlanta. When Eugene exited the interstate, Bobbi sat on the edge of her seat admiring the familiar shops and buildings, and the crowds moving swiftly down the sidewalk. Every time she came home it seemed like something new and exciting was happening. Hotlanta was definitely a thriving city, and one of the more popular major markets in the country.

Eugene pulled up to the curb. "We're here, Miss Farqua." He exited the car and walked around to let Bobbi out. He extended his hand.

She put her hand in his and stepped out. Her eyes traveled up the impressive ten story building. The smoke gray tinted glass design made the structure resemble a huge mirror. Although she had passed it by many times before, she had never actually been inside.

"Good luck with your meeting," he said, handing her the bag he had laid on the backseat.

"Thanks, Eugene. See you soon." She took the handle of her rolling bag and walked towards the building.

The lobby was amazing. Polished marble floors and chrome fixtures dominated the space. There were people walking around, some casually with coffee in hand while others were rushing by.

Probably late for work, Bobbi thought. There were others already waiting at the elevator bank so she joined them and continued to admire the building's amenities. From her purview, she could see a dry cleaners, a gift shop and café on her right, and it looked like business offices to her left.

When the elevator doors opened everyone stepped inside. Bobbi asked for the tenth floor to know one in particular since she wasn't close enough to the panel to select it herself.

The elevator was crowded and Bobbi could tell the men were checking her out. She smiled to herself. How could she blame them? Even though she didn't consider herself conceited, she knew she was simply stunning today. If Terry Barnes wasn't sure about hiring her company to handle his publicity needs, one look at her in this suit would bring clarity to his decision.

The old Bobbi would never consider playing up her looks and assets to get her way, especially in business, but her opinion of men was different now. Ultimately, they all only wanted one thing from women anyway, so she would play on Terry's weaknesses and all other men for that matter—business or otherwise—to her advantage. Don't hate the player, hate the game.

On the tenth floor—the penthouse—the elevator doors opened and Bobbi stepped out. Suite 1000, her destination, was the only suite on the floor. *Impressive,* she thought. A glass wall with huge glass double doors revealed a contemporary designed and furnished reception area. She went inside.

The floors were black marble just like in the lobby, the walls a light shade of gray. A plasma screen television hung on the wall across from the reception desk. In the center of the floor were a black sofa, two chairs and a large glass top coffee table.

"Good morning. May I help you?"

"Yes. Good morning. My name is Bobbi Farqua." Bobbi looked at her watch realizing she was forty-five minutes early. "I'm a bit early, but I have a ten thirty appointment with Mister Kendall."

The receptionist was cute. She appeared to be in her early twenties with cinnamon brown skin, and a pleasant smile. Her hair was styled short and spiked in the crown. She wore a low cut turquoise top. After their greeting she dialed Mister Kendall.

"Mister Kendall, your ten thirty appointment is here."

"Miss Farqua is here?" he asked. "She's early. Give me about ten minutes. I need to call Mr. Barnes to see if he can get here a little earlier. Tell her I'll be right out. Thanks, Tish."

The receptionist turned her attention back to Bobbi. "Please have a seat Miss Farqua—Mister Kendall will be with you shortly."

"Thanks." Bobbi picked up the June issue of *Black Enterprise* off the glass table and sat in one of the high-back chairs. With her bag next to her on the floor and her reptile print handbag in the chair with her, she crossed her legs and flipped through the pages. Being an entrepreneur required dedication, commitment, and bringing your "A" game to every business deal. Competing with the big dogs in corporate America didn't allow her the luxury of a bad day or being ill prepared for any reason. So even though she was turning pages in a magazine right now, she was in the zone. The only thing on her mind was explaining why My Way Communications was the only choice for Terry.

"Bobbi Farqua?" Jim extended his hand to Bobbi as she stood. "Jim Kendall."

"Yes, Jim. How are you?" she responded, with a smile and firm hand shake. "Finally, we meet."

Jim chuckled. “I know. It took many conversations to get to this point. But we’re here now. If you’re ready, let’s go back to my office.”

Bobbi grabbed her things and followed Jim out of the reception area through another set of double glass doors into the main office space. They chatted about her flight on the way to his office.

This was Bobbi’s first time meeting Jim in person so she was checking him out. He wasn’t fine by her definition but he was an attractive man in an intelligent, confident kind of way. The gray suit he had on was impeccable on his athletic frame. His hair was thinning on top and cut low. His smile lit up the room.

“By the way, thanks for sending your driver. It was such a relief not to be concerned about a rental car and dealing with traffic. Eugene was great.”

“No problem. I’m glad it worked out for you. I’ll call Eugene once the meeting is over so he’ll be waiting for you when–”

The phone rang interrupting him just as they entered his office. “Just one minute.” He moved quickly around his desk to answer it, and motioned for Bobbi to have a seat.

“Yes, Tish?”

“Mister Barnes is here.”

“Thanks. Tell him to come on back.”

Chapter 7

Bobbi admired Jim's office while he talked on the phone. Shades of burgundy and tan were the back drop for his oversized mahogany desk and huge black leather executive chair trimmed in mahogany wood. The essence was masculine.

When he hung up with Tish he walked around his desk to sit on the corner near Bobbi. He told her that Terry was on his way back and that after introductions the three of them would move to the conference room for their meeting.

The door was slightly ajar when Terry reached Jim's office so he knocked once and stepped inside. He saw Jim first, then the striking woman sitting in front of him. *Was this Bobbi Farqua? Damn.*

"What's up man?" Terry said. He greeted Jim with a solid hand shake and that brotherly hug men give one another with a firm pat on the back.

"What's up man? Glad you could make it. I'd like to introduce you to Bobbi Farqua, the owner of My Way Communications." Jim looked at Bobbi.

"And Bobbi, meet Terry Barnes, star quarterback for the Atlanta Condors.

Terry turned towards Bobbi and extended his hand. "A pleasure to meet you, Miss Farqua."

Bobbi stood, presenting all five-ten of her stature in stilettos. She smiled at the handsome quarterback and shook his hand. He wasn't much talker than her. Casually dressed, he wore blue jeans, a fashionable white t-shirt with a spread eagle design on the front, and a tan sports jacket. A thinly trimmed beard outlined his round face. His hair was cut low.

"Please call me Bobbi. The pleasure is all mine. Thanks for taking the time to meet with me today."

"And call me Terry."

Their hand shake was firm and quick. Not at all representative of his initial reaction to her just seconds ago when she was sitting down. The raise of his brow when he glanced her way while greeting Jim had not gone unnoticed to her. But this was a professional setting, so she wouldn't hold his seemingly disinterested demeanor against him. After all, she didn't mind working hard to win him over. Game on. He would be eating out of her hands by the time the meeting wrapped up.

Beauty and brains afforded a woman infinite possibilities in the business world, especially with men. And both were Bobbi's strong suits. Since all of her initial transactions with potential clients took place over the phone, she had the opportunity to leverage her business acumen without her looks getting in the way. Once she piqued their interest enough to schedule an in-person presentation, it was a done deal. This meeting with Terry would be no different.

In the conference room Jim and Terry took a seat at the huge table with seating for twenty while Bobbi prepared for her presentation. She set up her laptop and used her portable projector to display her presentation on the overhead projection screen. Walking to the front of the table opposite her audience, she opened her presentation with an anecdote. And it worked. Terry and Jim both laughed. She giggled inside when the two men looked at each other as if to say this girl is alright.

Now that Terry was primed for what she had to say, for the next thirty minutes Bobbi talked about her company's capabilities. She showed Terry a personalized snapshot of how she thought he would be best served by her services. Judging the look on his face, she knew no other PR firm had provided him with as much detail and showed genuine concern for his career and image as she had. This was her niche. It was all about the client.

For good measure and to take the energy in the room up a notch, she unbuttoned her suit jacket and rested her hand on her small waist as she continued talking. Terry's dark eyes which seemed to be focused on her mouth for most of the meeting were now tuned in to her mid-section. She smiled inside. Men were so predictable.

Bobbi walked towards the gentlemen as she concluded the meeting. "So you see Terry, My Way Communications is positioned to represent you no matter what your PR needs may be. I will personally manage your account—with input from you of course—and stand ready to represent you at a moments notice." With her final words, she joined them at the table, sitting next to Terry. She glanced across the table at Jim then turned her full attention to Terry. "Do you have any questions for me?"

"I'm impressed. You really did your homework." His tone was genuine. "But I do have a question for you though. You said your firm handles urban entertainment type clients. How many clients do you have and who are they?

"I'm glad you asked." She reached inside her bag and pulled out a folder. "Here's a list of my clients and their telephone numbers. They have agreed to answer any questions you have about services I've provided them. So they are more than willing to engage you."

Terry slowly nodded his approval. "Thanks, Bobbi." He looked at Jim, then back at Bobbi.

There was a silent pause so Bobbi took control again.

"Terry. Here's my business card. Take your time and check out my company and my credentials. And when you're ready, give me a call." Bobbi began shutting down her equipment while Terry read over her client list and Jim made small talk with her about the meeting.

Terry stood to excuse himself, telling Jim that he needed to see him for a moment after he used the restroom. But before he left the room he turned to Bobbi to thank her for coming to Atlanta to meet with him. He reached for her hand and squeezed it gently.

"I'll definitely be in touch within the week to discuss my intentions. It's truly been my pleasure meeting you. Have a safe trip back to DC." He squeezed her hand again, and just like that, with a quick nod towards Jim, he was out the door.

Well that was strange, Bobbi thought. But men could be strange cookies sometimes. Dealing with them in business wasn't much different than dealing with them on a personal level. Bobbi finished packing her things. Through her peripheral she could see Jim watching her every move.

"So, Bobbi. I may have some other business to throw your way if you're interested. I like your style—the way you handle business. From what I just saw here this morning, Terry should be ready to sign on the dotted line today, I know I would be. But if for some reason he needs persuading I'll be the first to do so. You're thorough and I think you would provide the perfect representation for him."

Bobbi smiled. "Thanks for the vote of confidence," she smiled, zipping her bag closed. "I'm sure Terry will make the right decision for him. But as for your other clients, give me a call so we can discuss there needs and we'll go from there." Bobbi stood up ready to leave.

"Sounds good to me." Jim stood to his feet. "Just a minute, Bobbi. Let me call for Eugene." He used the telephone in the conference room to call Tish and have her notify Eugene that Bobbi would be down shortly. After ending the call, Jim escorted Bobbi back to the reception area.

Her return flight to DC didn't leave until seven o'clock that night. She had planned it that way so she would have time for a late lunch and visit with her mom. Jim knew about her plans and had graciously agreed to provide the driver for her trip to see her mom as well as back to the airport.

Jim held Bobbi's right hand in both of his. "Thanks for everything. I'll be in touch real soon.

"And thank you for everything—especially the driver." Bobbi smiled and waved good-bye to both Jim and Tish.

Chapter 8

On her way to see her mom in Buckhead, an affluent upscale community in Atlanta, she carefully dissected her meeting with Terry and Jim. The fact that Terry hadn't committed to a contract immediately had thrown her slightly off balance. She had expected him to sign on the dotted line without hesitation.

Although she didn't question her abilities where business was concerned, she couldn't lie that it was a minor set-back to her ego. After all, she expected men to respond to her, period. Whether she reciprocated their interest or not was irrelevant.

Maybe Terry didn't find her attractive. *Nah, that's not it.* Bobbi chuckled. There she was over analyzing things. Through the grapevine she'd heard that he was engaged or married anyway so she wasn't interested in him romantically—she just wanted his business.

Bobbi checked her speculating behavior right there. Her thoughts would be better spent focused on her plans for the rest of the day. Terry said he would call with his answer so that was that. Bobbi reached in her purse for her Blackberry and called her mom to let her know she was en route.

"Hello."

"Hey, ma! What are you doing?"

"Hey, sweetie. I'm in my office working, and waiting to hear from you. Are you on your way?"

"Yep. I should be there in about fifteen minutes," Bobbi confirmed looking at her watch.

"Okay. Use your key and let yourself in. I'll be here in my office when you get here.

"Yes, ma'am. See you in a few." Bobbi ended the call.

Bobbi had briefly seen her mom in New York on Mother's Day weekend. Daren, Grace's husband of four years had surprised her with the trip and asked Bobbi to come celebrate with them if she could. So after attending a week long conference in Los Angeles, Bobbi changed her flight arrangements to fly into New York instead of back to DC. She hung out with her mom and stepfather all day that Saturday and most of Sunday before catching a flight home. That was only a month ago; however she really looked forward to hanging out with her today.

When Bobbi arrived at her mom's house, she told Eugene she'd call him around four o'clock to let him know where to pick her up. She took her things and went inside. Grace was still in her office working.

"What's crackin' ma?" Bobbi walked over to where Grace sat behind a large cherry wood desk and kissed her on the cheek.

Grace looked at Bobbi above the rim of her reading glasses. "Hey, sunshine." She leaned into Bobbi's kiss.

For the next thirty minutes they doted over the other's hair, clothes, skin, and make-up—the usual girly stuff—like they hadn't seen one another in years.

Grace was an elegant, seasoned older version of Bobbi—minus the green eyes. She wore her hair in a chin length honey blond bob with lighter highlights. Though her figure had thickened with age, it still held its hour glass shape.

Suddenly a rumbling in Bobbi's stomach reminded her that it was lunchtime. And she knew exactly where she wanted to go—

Leonard's Grille on Peachtree Road. They had the best seafood in town.

"Mom, let's go to Leonard's Grille. I have a taste for crab cakes." Bobbi followed her mom to the kitchen.

"Leonard's Grille?" Grace asked. "Fairview Towers is only four or five blocks from there. I could have met you downtown if that's where we're going." Grace grabbed a picture of water from the refrigerator and two glasses from the cupboard.

"Honestly, I didn't think about it before now," said Bobbi after she drank all of her water. "All I was focused on was coming to the house after my meeting."

"Well, Leonard's it is. Crab cake sounds good to me." Grace finished her water and grabbed her keys and purse. "Let's ride."

Bobbi laughed at her moms comment. She told her mom to go ahead and get the car and she would lock up after she put the glasses in the dishwasher. So Grace headed for the garage.

Moments later Grace pulled around front with the top down on her silver two-seater convertible Benz and Bobbi jumped in. But not before putting her carry-on bag in the small trunk and removing her suit jacket to lay it across her lap.

"I see you're keeping the car clean," Bobbi complimented. It was Grace's Christmas gift from Daren last year.

Grace smiled at her daughter. "Daren keeps this car clean. You know that's not my thing."

"Show you right, Gracie," Bobbi replied and put on her shades.

Grace laughed at Bobbi and pulled off into the warm June afternoon. Wind blowing through their hair, other than the Gospel music playing on the radio, they rode in silence.

Once she exited the highway and could actually hear herself talk, Grace asked Bobbi about her meeting. Bobbi told her that the presentation went extremely well, however, Terry needed time to think about his decision. She told her that he said he would call with an answer in a couple of days.

At a stop light Grace turned to Bobbi and patted her thigh. “He’ll call.” Grace let her eyes travel over her beautiful daughter from head to toe. “Trust me. He’ll call.”

Leonard’s Grille was packed. Bobbi and Grace walked inside the popular restaurant and stopped short of the hostess stand to decide if they wanted to wait for a table. Overhearing their conversation, the striking hostess with dark hair and sapphire blue eyes told them that the wait was only ten minutes. So the mother and daughter nodded in agreement to stay. Bobbi gave her name to the hostess and they went to sit on the leather bench near the entrance.

Within five minutes they were being escorted to a table. The majority of the patrons they walked by were in business attire. The way they lingered around laughing and talking, they must not want to go back to work, Bobbi thought.

Seated, Bobbi and Grace looked over the menu even though they already knew what they wanted. A chubby waitress with a short burgundy afro took their drink order. Both ladies ordered raspberry iced tea and told the waitress they were ready to place their food order as well.

“Okay. What would you like?” the waitress asked in a thick Mother Land accent.

“I’ll have crab cakes with grilled asparagus.” Bobbi’s mouth watered just thinking about the well seasoned mostly crab meat entrée. They hardly used any filler.

Grace handed the waitress her menu. “I’ll have the same.”

The waitress brought their raspberry teas to the table, smiled and left.

While they waited for lunch, Grace filled Bobbi in on all the latest happenings with the family and around the neighborhood. Bobbi couldn't help but smile watching her mom's animated gestures as she shared details about her neighbors. Since Grace still lived in the same house they moved into when Bobbi was ten, the neighbors were like family. Literally, the group of friends got together every Saturday night for dinner and trash talking. Like most families, they laughed, talked, and on occasion, even cried together.

To Bobbi, her mom was an amazing woman and an unwavering source of encouragement. Spending time with her like they were today was a bright spot in Bobbi's life; especially since they lived so far apart. Usually, Bobbi made it home about six times a year, but that wasn't always enough.

The waitress returned with their lunch plates and asked if they needed anything else.

"Can we get refills?" Bobbi smiled and nodded towards their glasses.

"Sure." The waitress left the table with their glasses in hand.

"By the way, how's Nikki doing?" Grace asked before she put a fork full of crab meat in her mouth. The last time Grace talked to Nikki she was studying hard to pass her second Bar Exam to become a licensed attorney in Maryland. But she wanted to hear from Bobbi just how her Godchild was doing. Nikki was pushing herself really hard and her mom and dad, as well as Grace were concerned that she was overdoing it.

"She's doing fine. I talked to her last night. Besides being tired from studying all day and night, she's okay. She said she can rest after she passes the Bar next week. But I plan to drag her out of the house this weekend to have dinner or go out for drinks."

The waitress returned with their refills.

"Good," said Grace. "And make sure you do that because whether she realizes it or not her brain could use a break."

"No worries, ma. I got this," she teased.

Daren called to check on Grace during lunch. He never let her go too far without making sure she was okay. Bobbi took the opportunity while her mom was on the phone to check her e-mails. She had a few messages from her assistant, Cierra, but they could wait until she was on her way to the airport.

After lunch, Bobbi had a couple of hours to spare before she needed to head for the airport. So she and Grace strolled down Peachtree Road window shopping mostly, when Grace saw a scarf she couldn't live without. They went inside the quaint boutique with soft pink and beige décor to get a closer look. The tinkling bell above the door announced their entry.

"Welcome to Sadie's. Let me know if I can help you with anything," said the perky sales clerk. Her hair was pulled back in a bun so tight her eyes looked like they were stretched to the sides of her face.

"Hi." Both Bobbi and Grace smiled.

Grace walked over to check out the scarf while Bobbi went in the opposite direction towards a clothing rack with summer suits. Bobbi took off her shades, resting them on top of her head, and flipped through the designer garments. Image was everything so it really was important to buy quality fabric with quality workmanship; however, the prices in this store were ridiculous, Bobbi thought.

Bobbi looked over at her mom. Grace wasn't just looking at scarves now, she was trying on shoes. Bobbi smiled and shook her head. In her family, shopping was definitely a generational curse.

Bobbi checked her watch and realized it was about time for her to be leaving for the airport. So she whipped out her Blackberry and called Eugene, telling him to meet her at Leonard's Grille. Then she walked over to see if her mom was ready to go. Before they left, Grace purchased two pairs of shoes, the matching hand bags, and the scarf from the window.

Mother and daughter walked back towards Grace's car to wait for Eugene. As if they planned it, Eugene pulled up to the curb just as Grace and Bobbi walked up to her convertible. So Bobbi took her laptop bag out of the trunk and Grace threw hers in.

Bobbi told her mom goodbye, hugged and kissed her and made her way over to the black Towne car. Eugene helped her inside and they were on their way.

Chapter 9

I-85 South was bumper to bumper traffic. Once again Bobbi was grateful to Jim for offering her a driver. Her flight didn't leave for two hours so she wasn't too worried. Even with traffic they should be at the airport within thirty minutes.

Bobbi kicked off her heels and wiggled her toes. She took a deep breath and nestled into the soft leather seat. Completely relaxed, she wondered what her man was doing. She laughed. Using the words, "her man" was such a strong way to express what he really was to her.

Actually, Tony was more like her convenient lover. Between them, there was no commitment or expectations. If her libido went into overdrive she called him up, and likewise. He was always a willing participant. And fortunately for her, his sex drive matched hers so she didn't have to rely on more than one man to satisfy her needs; although she had her backups.

Oddly though, she genuinely enjoyed hanging with Tony—going to movies, dinner, or whatever. She even asked him to accompany her to social and business functions when she wanted a date.

She knew their arrangement probably made Tony feel like the M-A-N. After all, what man wouldn't want a dime piece who kept her emotions in check, preferring non committal sex to a meaningful relationship? But the truth of the matter was this was the perfect arrangement for Bobbi, and that's the only reason he had his cake and ate it too.

Long gone were the days of being heart broken over a man who wouldn't be faithful to her no matter how hard she loved him. The where-is-this-relationship-going question was one thing Tony never had to worry about hearing from her mouth. Just as men avoided that question like the bubonic plague, so did she. Love didn't live here anymore.

A call came in on her Blackberry. "Hey Nik, what's good?"

"Hey B. Nothing—just chillin'. You know why I'm calling so give it up. How'd the meeting with Mister NFL go?" chimed Nikki's perky voice.

"You know I worked it girl. I blew it out the water. Terry didn't sign the contract today like I thought he would be I have a gut feeling that he will. I think he's holding out, but it's all good. I hope to hear something by the end of the week. But on another note, Jim Kendall, Terry's agent was cool. He actually wants to do more business together so I expect to hear from him again real soon."

"I know you represented, diva. What was Terry like though? Was he as fine in person?"

"Hell to the yeah. But I think he's engaged or maybe even married. At least that's what I heard. We didn't have a chance for small talk so–"

"Nik, let me call you back. I have another call coming in."

"Peace. Call me tomorrow," replied Nikki before hanging up.

"Bobbi Farqua," she answered.

"Hello Bobbi. This is Jim. Are you at the airport yet?

"Hi, Jim. Not yet. We're getting there but you know how crazy this traffic is during rush hour.

"Yeah, I do. Well I called to tell you that I talked with Terry after you left and he has a few more questions for you."

"Okay. Is he there with you now?"

"No. He left not long after you did this morning. I didn't want to interrupt your plans for the day so I waited until now to call."

"I appreciate the consideration. I'll have my assistant call your office first thing tomorrow morning to arrange a conference call."

"Sounds great, Bobbi. Safe travels."

"Thanks, Jim...for everything. Talk to you tomorrow. Goodbye."

"Bam!" Bobbi said aloud, grinning from here to Africa. Terry having more questions was definitely a promising indication that he was ready to make a decision. Her thoughts immediately went to what signing him would mean for her company's appeal to future clients of his caliber. Life was golden!

Her reverie quickly turned naughty as the familiar tug between her legs took her thoughts in a different direction. Suddenly, she was horny. There was something about closing business deals that toyed with her hormones. Perhaps it was the excitement, or maybe a sense of fulfillment in her work that caused her body to respond in this way. She squeezed her thighs together. Just as soon as she was settled in at her boarding gate she would call Tony to make plans for a midnight rendezvous.

Chapter 10

Bobbi pulled out her Blackberry and called Tony. He answered on the second ring.

"Hey love," he said in his deep sexy voice. "Where are you?"

"Hey baby," she replied in a tone just as sexy. "I'm at the airport on my way back home. Can you come over tonight?"

"What time do you think you'll be home?" Tony asked. "I have an early day tomorrow. Remember the murder trial I told you about? We go to court in the morning so if I come I'll need to get dressed and leave from your house."

"Okay, that's cool." Bobbi checked her watch. "You can come over at eleven thirty." She figured that would give her plenty of time to get herself together. "But when you leave in the morning please don't wake me up. I need to catch up on some sleep," she said. "And oh..." Bobbi giggled. "Don't wear any underwear. I don't want anything in my way."

Tony shook his head and laughed. "You just be ready when I get there." Tony didn't know any other woman like Bobbi. She was aggressive at the right times, fun to be around, she loved sex, and there was no drama with her. How could one man get so lucky? "Have a safe trip love. I'll see you tonight."

Just the sound of his voice was pushing her over the edge. "Yes you will, daddy. Bye," she whispered. Why couldn't she be home already?

Bobbi and Tony had been dating for over two years. A mutual business associate recommended that Bobbi consult with Tony for legal advice concerning her company and client contracts. Once their business was finished, Tony asked her out and they had been seeing each other ever since.

Neither one of them ever felt the need to pressure the other about their relationship. They both enjoyed being single and free to date other people. That's just how Bobbi wanted it and obviously so did Tony. However, when they came together it was explosive. Because they both had demanding, stressful careers they used each other physically and mentally to release, unwind, and unload. And tonight would be no different.

Preparing for her meeting with Terry, like all presentations for prospective clients, had taken long hours and a lot of work. So she was sleep deprived, and now seriously horny. Sleep she would take care of on the plane but as for the latter… Tony was in for the ride of his life, literally.

Chapter 11

Bobbi boarded the plane, stowed her carry-on and took her seat. It had been a full, productive day. She fastened her seatbelt and closed her eyes. Her lips turned up in a smile. Finally, she could count sheep until she drifted off into lah-lah-land.

"Excuse me, is that seat taken?"

There was no response.

"Miss. Excuse me," came the male voice again.

Bobbi's eyes popped open. She thought she was dreaming. Standing in the aisle next to her pointing at the window seat on her row was the sexy ass brother from her morning flight.

Bobbi pointed her finger towards her chest. "You talking to me?"

"Yes. Is that seat taken…the window seat?" He asked for the second time still pointing.

Today was truly a great day, Bobbi reflected. First there was the ground breaking meeting with Terry; then spending the day with her mom; the anticipation of Tony scratching her itch in a few hours, and now this.

Bobbi looked around at the other vacant seats on the plane wondering why he'd chosen her row. She hunched her shoulders.

"Uh...I don't guess so," she finally said.

He proceeded to secure his belongings in the overhead compartment and side stepped past her to the window seat. “Thanks,” he said after he was seated.

Bobbi smiled and nodded in his direction then closed her eyes again. Her head against the seat, thoughts of Tony were slowly fading into the shadows of curiosity with her new travel companion. And for the second time today she wondered what his story was.

As soon as he was settled, her new travel mate made a call on his cell phone. Bobbi tried not to listen to his conversation but it wasn’t working. She was way too nosey and interested in who he was to mind her own business. Based on his tone she could tell that he was talking to a woman. But it was the unmistakable way he said “I love you” before ending the call that confirmed he was romantically involved with someone.

As the flight attendant prepared the cabin for take-off, Bobbi glanced over at her travel mate and smiled. Game recognized game. His expression of endearment on the phone was just as much for Bobbi as it was for his woman. It was his way of checking Bobbi; to put her on notice that he already had a first lady in his life. So no matter how well they became acquainted on the flight, he wasn’t looking for anything special.

But this psychology was nothing new to Bobbi. There was a reason he sat next to her with all the open seats around them; he was just as curious about her as she was him. So let the games begin.

Chapter 12

Thanks to ol' what's his name sitting to her left, sleep was the furthest thing on Bobbi's mind. So after the pilot announced the altitude and turned off the fasten seatbelt light, she went to the restroom to freshen up. When she returned to her seat, the handsome traveler took the opportunity to introduce himself.

"By the way, my name is Savon—Savon Turner." He extended his hand to greet her then continued. "Didn't you take the seven o'clock flight this morning?"

Check mate. Bobbi reached across the center seat to shake his hand. "Hi Savon, nice to meet you. I'm Bobbi Farqua. And yes, I do remember you from this morning." Savon's hand held hers seconds longer than it should have considering he had a woman.

After introductions, there was an awkward silence between them. However, it didn't bother Bobbi. She was curious but not desperate. If he didn't say another word the entire flight neither would she.

But Savon didn't feel the same way. There were things about Bobbi he wanted to know so he made small talk. He asked if she lived in DC and what she did for a living. When she told him that she was raised in Buckhead from the age of ten he just stared at her.

"Small world," he said. "What part?"

"Peachtree Park. Why?" asked Bobbi.

"So was I—on the North side. My family moved there when I was in eighth grade."

"No way!" Bobbi looked at him closer—her head slightly tilted. But she still didn't recognize him. "Humph. I've never seen you."

"You don't look familiar either," he replied.

They talked about their neighborhoods and growing up in Atlanta. When the name dropping started—the who's who up in the hood—they discovered they had mutual acquaintances.

"Talk about coincidences," Bobbi offered.

"Yeah." Savon had a far off look in his eyes. "So do you follow professional sports?"

"A little. I usually go to a few games during the season—football and basketball. But I prefer basketball. It's more exciting."

"I see…" said Savon.

"The Washington Warriors have sucked for the last couple of years. I mean I'm a football fan and all but sometimes I want to shake'm up real good when they loose games they should have had in the bag.

Savon frowned. "I play for the Warriors." There was a tinge of disappointment in his voice. "Actually I was invited to Atlanta to do an interview on a sports talk show. I also visited my old high school and passed out signed photographs. If you were a fan I would have signed one for you."

"Excuse me, can I get you something to drink?" the brunette flight attendant interrupted. Her make-up was way overdone. She smiled revealing lipstick on her front teeth.

Both Savon and Bobbi asked for water. The attendant scribbled on her pad and moved on.

Although Bobbi felt a bit guilty about her Warriors comment, she was only voicing her opinion. She picked the conversation back up where they left off.

"Don't get me wrong, Savon, I definitely consider myself a Warriors fan, but come on…you guys could do much better. My girlfriend and I have a running joke that maybe the team should consider group hypnosis to figure out why they can't win."

Savon looked at her like she had three heads. This chic was bold, he thought.

Realizing that her attempt at humor didn't go over too well, Bobbi tried to smooth things over by changing the subject.

To answer one of his earlier questions, she told him that she was a publicist. They talked about her line of work and about making money. When the flight attendant rolled by with their waters and two bags of peanuts, it gave Bobbi an opportunity to shift the conversation.

She asked him about his social life and where he hung out. Conversation flowed easily between them and before they knew it the pilot interrupted the cabin with an announcement to prepare for landing.

In the time it took to fly from Atlanta to DC, Bobbi could feel the chemistry grow between them like a wild vine. During their conversation, Savon told Bobbi that he had a fiancée so she knew this meeting was both the beginning and the end of her curiosity. He was officially off limits. Bobbi didn't put herself in situations where she had to creep or sneak around. Ducking and dodging the next woman just wasn't her style. Plus, she refused to argue or fight over any man.

As the plane landed neither of them said a word. They had talked the entire flight about everything including relationships, and how hard it was to stay true to one person. Now in their silence, a thousand thoughts passed through Bobbi's mind about meeting the perfect stranger.

Exiting the aircraft, the two walked down the concourse and out of the airport together. When they made it to the set of elevators for the parking garage things became awkward. If he wasn't damn near married, Bobbi would have known what say. And Savon knew he would be asking for trouble if he went with his attraction to her and asked if they could hang out sometime.

Bobbi broke the silence. She reached in her purse for a business card. "Here." She handed him her card. "If you're ever in the market for a publicist give me a call."

He examined the card rubbing his thumb over it. He looked at Bobbi. "You didn't tell me you were the owner of the PR firm where you work." He tapped the card against his finger. "Hmmm. I'm impressed." *Brains and beauty in one package. Damn.*

Once again there was a pregnant pause between them. Then simultaneously, they began to speak. They both said how great it was to have someone to talk to on the two hour flight.

For Bobbi, their meeting was too comfortable. They knew some of the same people; grew up in the same town, and talking to him was easy. It was like chillin' with an old friend.

She looked up at him. When their eyes met, something inside of her connected with him. Now she knew she had to bounce.

"Well Savon, it's been a long day. My bed is calling me." She smiled. "But it's been such a pleasure meeting you and reminiscing about home–"

He cut her off. "Check it out. A few of my boys are coming to DC to hang out with me this weekend. We'll be at Club Dream, Friday night in VIP. You should come." Bobbi tried not to read into his invitation. After all she couldn't have what she really wanted from his fine ass any way.

She turned to press the button to take her to level three where she parked then looked back at Savon. "If I can, I'll stop by for a drink with my girl." The ding from the elevator was like music to her ears. As soon as the doors opened she stepped inside. She needed to get as far away from this delicious man as she could. "Remember…call me if you need a publicist. Take care, Savon," she said before the doors closed.

Chapter 13

Bobbi checked the water before stopping up the tub and adding fruit scented bubbles to her bath. Candles burned throughout the house as *Maxwell* crooned *This Woman's Work* in repeat mode in the CD changer. For reasons she couldn't explain, this song made her feel ultra sexy and uninhibited.

She pulled her hair back and pinned it up with a clip. "Ahhh," she said when she stepped in the hot foamy water. She leaned back and closed her eyes, letting the melody and gentleness of Maxwell's voice relax her senses.

She smiled. Tony hated this song because she played it almost every time he came over. "Who plays the same damn song in repeat mode for three hours, B?" he would ask. Bobbi laughed.

She took her time cleaning the days grit and sweat from two different climates off of her body. Twenty minutes later she stepped out of the tub refreshed and ready for Tony. After drying off, she smoothed on Pomegranate body lotion and went into her bedroom to find something to wear. Flipping through her lingerie drawer she pulled out a tiny black lace thong and smiled. "Guess this is it," she said aloud.

She walked into the closet and scanned the boxes of shoes with Polaroid pictures taped on front. A pair of high-heeled ankle strap black sandals with a black flower near the toe was her choice. She grabbed them from the box and went to sit on the chaise lounge in her room to fasten the straps. A quick glance at the alarm clock next to her bed reminded her that Tony would be there in less than fifteen minutes.

So she went into the bathroom to finish getting herself together. Humming along to her favorite get freaky song, she applied very little black eye-liner, mascara, and sheer pink lip gloss. She released her hair from the clip then brushed it neatly into place. She made sure she let the sides fall over the front of her shoulders to rest on her bare breasts. “Perfect,” she said looking in the mirror with a mischievous twinkle in her eyes. Everything was ready: the candles, the music, the wine chilling in the freezer, and now her.

Bobbi tidied her room and headed downstairs to the kitchen. She took the wine out of the freezer and grabbed two flutes from the cupboard. *This woman's work is about to go down until I'm satisfied or passed out - one of the two.* She laughed at her silly thought.

Just as she uncorked the bottle the doorbell rang. She filled the glasses and went to the door. When she opened it Tony stood speechless.

“Hi baby,” Bobbi said seductively, handing him one of the flutes. She reached for his free hand and pulled him inside then closed and locked the door.

“Damn, B.” Tony let his overnight bag slide from his shoulder to the floor. Bobbi was fine as hell. And she knew how to keep a man coming back for more. He sipped his wine then set it on the table near the door.

He reached for her hips and pulled her to him. He kissed her slow at first, tasting her tongue and suckling her bottom lip. Then the kiss became hungry. Bobbi’s wine glass crashed to the floor when she threw her arms around his neck. Tony's hands where all over her, and she loved it. He backed her up against the wall for support, and then his tongue traveled from her lips to her neck to her breast, her belly—then to that spot. She couldn't take it anymore. So she pulled on his arms so he could stand up. Then she undid his pants and reached inside for what she wanted, and smiled. It was solid as a rock. She grabbed his hand and pulled him over to the sofa where she straddled him and rode her way to ecstasy.

Chapter 14

Tony didn't wake Bobbi when he left for work the next morning. He just smiled down at her naked body sound asleep—the results of his handy work. Last night until the wee hours of the morning, he had given her one orgasm after the next until she drifted off to sleep.

Last night, when she opened the door and he heard *A Woman's Work* playing in the background, he knew what time it was. Whenever Bobbi played that old ass *Maxwell* CD it meant she was horny as hell and on a mission. So initially he let her take control, but after that first round he had set the pace and led the way to a night full of pleasure for them both.

On his way to work, Tony thought about his relationship with Bobbi. It had been more than two years since they started hanging out and he still couldn't believe how good he had it with her. He had definitely hit the jackpot. This woman was no doubt a head turner; any man would want her on his arm. Her body made a man weak in the knees, and she was successful in her own right.

But what made him the luckiest man in the universe was the fact that she didn't act like a woman. Sure, she was feminine and lady-like, but those characteristics and qualities that can drive a man away were non existent in Bobbi. She never complained or nagged if he didn't call her every day, or even ask if he was seeing someone else. Emotions didn't rule her life. For that reason alone she could get anything she wanted from him. Bobbi was his homey, lover, friend.

His lips turned up at the corners as he pulled into the parking garage at the courthouse. He wished he could clone Bobbi. Just thinking about all the stress free, freaky, no ties sex he could be having if all women were like her made his nature rise.

Tony was a successful attorney in Washington DC. After practicing law for only five years, he was on the fast track to becoming junior partner with his firm. He was thirty-years-old, handsome, well dressed, intelligent, resourceful, and had a street-edge.

His skin was like dark chocolate; his teeth were perfectly straight. He wore a goatee and his hair was cut low with brushed in waves. Suits hung like a dream on his well proportioned gym body.

Although Tony was extremely good at his work, there was no question that his good looks went a long way with women, especially his female colleagues and clients. Bobbi was his girl no doubt, and he loved spending time with her without the constant demands of a commitment being thrown at him. But the fact remained that he was a very eligible bachelor who took pride in upholding the essence of what that meant: to get as much ass as he could, when you could, and how he could. Of course that would only be quality ass for him because he was a quality guy. That's why he and Bobbi fit so well together.

It was Saturday morning and Bobbi lay in bed; her thoughts reflective over the past week. Yesterday, the fruits of her labor had finally paid off with Terry Barnes. True to his word he had called on Wednesday with more questions about her services and said that he wanted her to be his publicist. Since he already had plans to come to DC on Friday, he said he would stop by her office to sign the contract before the day was out, and he did.

Terry was much more personable this time. He invited her to a late lunch after signing the contract and Bobbi accepted. During lunch she found out that he was indeed engaged, and that overall he was a descent guy. But before he dropped her back off at work, he cast his fishing line to see if she would bite. He gave her his personal cell phone number—the same number she would imagine he'd already provided in the paper work he filled out a few hours ago—and told her to call him if she needed anything. And he stressed the word "anything". Typical, she thought.

So before she climbed out of his rented Tahoe, she smiled at him and said how pleased she was to have him as a client. He smiled back at her, holding the hand that she had extended as a farewell gesture, and didn't let go. He just stared at Bobbi with a weird smile on his face. So with her free hand she patted his hand that held hers and said she needed to get back to the office. She thanked him for lunch and opened the door for a quick exit. When he saw that, he let her hand go saying he'd be in touch. Terry was definitely a strange cookie.

Bobbi rolled over and looked at the clock. It was six thirty. She still had an hour before she had to get up. So her thoughts went back to her work week.

Jim had called on Thursday to set-up meetings with her so

she could fly to Atlanta and talk with a few of his clients. There was a definite quality about Jim that interested Bobbi. He was a man of his word and had been intentional in every transaction she'd had with him so far. That turned her on. She didn't see a wedding ring on his finger but of course that meant nothing in this day and time. Maybe she'd see what was up with him when she went to Atlanta in a couple of weeks. It didn't hurt to have a boy toy in different area codes.

Then there was Savon, the Washington Warriors, tight end. *Whew. And his tight end was just right for her*. Why did he have to be engaged? She thoroughly enjoyed talking with him on the plane and wanted to know more about him. However, in her gut she knew that Savon was trouble. It had been years since a man stirred her up on the inside the way he did. Yes, she wondered how he would be in the bedroom, but that wasn't her first thought about him. She actually wanted to spend time getting to know who he was.

A deep sigh escaped her lips. If she were honest with herself, this man had the potential to make her go back on her no-men-with-drama rule.

But later for all that; Bobbi yawned and stretched. Finally, it was the weekend and she and Nikki had planned a girl's day out, starting with breakfast at Nikki's house.

Chapter 16

Red, chocolate brown, and other earth tone shades dominated Bobbi's modernly decorated bedroom. A king sized bed with a huge brown leather headboard was the main attraction with a half dozen decorative pillows thrown on it. The walls were painted in a warm shade of tan adorned with an array of African-American art pieces.

At seven o'clock Bobbi jumped out of bed, ready for her shop-a-thon with Nikki. She straightened up around the house, called her mom to say hello, and took a shower. After spraying on a fruity scented body splash, she wrapped a towel around her body, did her make-up and slicked her hair back in a ponytail.

She dressed in a pair of white capris and a lemon colored baby doll top. Comfortable wedged heel sandals finished her look—stilettos wouldn't work today. She put on silver hoop earrings, grabbed her Gucci purse and keys and left the house.

The morning air was fresh and the sun was hidden behind a big fluffy white cloud. Bobbi looked up and inhaled. It was a beautiful day. She went to the curb and rolled her garbage bin back to the garage then jumped in her white CLK 350 Coupe Benz and headed to Nikki's condo in the heart of DC.

She dialed Nikki as she got closer to let her know she was almost there.

"What's up B? You down stairs?"

"Not yet. But I should be there in about ten minutes. Hopefully I can find parking on the street. I don't want to park in the garage."

Nikki walked over to her living room window and looked down at the street level. "I see a few spaces at the curb right now so you should be good."

"Cool. See you in a few."

"Okay."

Bobbi parked out front and used the call box for Nikki to buzz her up. She knocked on the door.

"It's open," Nikki yelled from the kitchen.

The smell of buttermilk biscuits and sausage slammed Bobbi's senses as soon as she opened the door. She walked into the kitchen and saw Nikki taking a pan from the oven.

"Dang, girl. You chef'n it up in here, huh? Do I smell sausage and biscuits?"

"And you know it," she replied with home-girl attitude. "You know how we do in the dirty, dirty." Lips puckered, Nikki stuck her butt out and made it bounce up and down, at the same time pointing towards Bobbi's. "These here are southern butts, raised on meat and potatoes. Yogurt and oat bran won't do nothing to keep these things phat like we like'm. We need to eat like this every now and then to keep our weight up back there—you heard?"

Bobbi stuck her butt out and looked at it. "Show you right," she agreed. They both laughed.

Nikki put the food on the table and Bobbi grabbed glasses from the cupboard and orange juice from the refrigerator. Nikki blessed the food and they dug in.

Although Bobbi had talked to Nikki quite a few times since she returned from Atlanta, she still hadn't told her about meeting Savon. They both had been so busy lately there hadn't been enough time to really get into it. But now they had all day.

"These turkey links are delicious. Do you have grape jelly?" asked Bobbi.

"Yeah, look in the frig."

Bobbi got up and opened the refrigerator and saw peach preserves next to the jelly. So she grabbed it instead, got a knife and sat down.

"You didn't say you had peach preserves," Bobbi said spreading it on her open biscuit.

Nikki bit into a turkey link and looked at Bobbi. "That's because you didn't ask, diva."

"Anyway," Bobbi went on "I had an unusual experience when I flew to Atlanta on Tuesday. I met someone who plays for the Warriors. We were on the same flight that morning and that night. Crazy, right? Well come to find out he grew up in Peachtree Park. I don't remember him but he actually knows some of the same people we do." Bobbi sipped her juice.

Nikki wiped her mouth with a napkin. "What's his name?" she asked quizzically. "You know Gavin can give you the 4-1-1 on him."

Gavin was Nikki's cousin, and played for the Washington Warriors. He moved to DC three years ago when he was drafted out of college. He was their connection to the athlete scene, private parties, and other celebrity events happening around town.

"His name is Savon Turner."

"Oh yeah." Nikki said as if she knew him. "He was recently traded from the Condors."

"And how do you know that?"

"Gavin was talking about him last weekend."

"Oh. Well he's engaged anyway, so I don't need Gavin to check this one out."

Nikki thought she detected disappointment in her best friend's voice. So she asked a few questions to see if her intuition was on point. And it was.

It had been a long time since Bobbi had let her emotions lead the way with a man. Past hurts had caused her to close her heart off so she only dealt with men who she considered safe—those who only wanted sex. And unfortunately, Bobbi seemed to be comfortable with her chosen lifestyle. The only expectations she had of the men she dealt with was that they be considerate and respectful of her time, and give her sex when she wanted it. And if they couldn't handle the arrangement she dropped them like a bad habit.

Nikki truly hoped this Savon character wasn't the man to break through the wall around Bobbi's heart. But it was clear from the twinkle in Bobbi's eyes when she was telling her how they met that he had made quite an impression on her dear friend. Hopefully the fact that he was engaged would be enough to keep him away from Bobbi.

Bobbi went on to tell Nikki about the conversations she and Savon had on the flight and how fine he was. She didn't leave anything out—except for the fact that she couldn't get him out of her head. But that wasn't important. With any luck she wouldn't run into him again and whatever her curiosity was with him would diminish over time.

After breakfast, Bobbi cleaned the kitchen while Nikki dressed in a knee length sun dress and wedge heeled sandals.

“I’m ready,” said Nikki walking into the living room.

“Well let’s ride.” Bobbi got up off the sofa and picked up her purse and keys while Nikki turned off the television and lights and checked the stove.

Outside, they got in Bobbi’s car and immediately Nikki reached for the CD case.

“Girl, we need to listen to something to get us hyped for our shop-a-thon.” Nikki flipped through the plastic holders. “Bingo. We’re about to listen to some *T.I.*”

“Cool.” Bobbi said. Put it on *Whatever You Like*.”

Bobbi and Nikki cranked that song all the way to the mall, seat-dancing and singing to each other: You can have whatever you like…yeaahh.

Chapter 17

It was Saturday night and Bobbi and Nikki were hanging out to celebrate Nikki passing the Maryland State Bar. After practicing law in DC for three years, she was now a licensed attorney in Maryland too.

Indi Blu was the local hot spot in DC for the crowd who considered themselves part of the elite. The place didn't open until four P.M. but when it did, young professionals, athletes, and local celebrities swarmed in for happy hour almost every night of the week. It was unique in its design with neon blue tube lighting that ran along the base of the ceiling throughout the restaurant. Large booths lined the walls on one side of the restaurant with tables in the center while tables only, covered in white cloths were on the other side. But the bar area was the main attraction. Contemporary R&B played from speakers mounted in the walls and television monitors were mounted above the bar. Besides the stools at the bar, ten pub tables with more stools filled the crowded space.

The bar area was also used for patrons waiting to be seated at a table, which is where Bobbi and Nikki were hanging out. They were both dressed to turn heads. Bobbi wore a sexy black above the knee halter dress with strappy black sandals; her hair and make-up flawless. And Nikki, aka Miss Fabulosity, was blinging in a silver tube top dress and peep toe sling backs, rocking her signature sleek shoulder-length bob; make-up the mirror of perfection.

"Here's to you Attorney Barton." Bobbi lifted her apple martini in the air. "For persevering, sacrificing, and pressing your way in spite of the odds. I'm very proud of you." Their glasses clinked.

Nikki's eyes filled with tears. "Thank you."

Just then they heard "Bobbi, party of two" announced over the intercom. They guzzled down their drinks and went to the hostess stand. An attractive young man with olive skin and dark curly hair escorted them to a table on the booth side of the restaurant.

"Your server will be with you shortly," he said before leaving the table.

"Thanks." Both ladies smiled.

When the skinny waitress came to the table Bobbi and Nikki ordered their meals and more drinks. Bobbi ordered grilled shrimp and spinach with butternut squash, and Nikki ordered her favorite—Tilapia, over a bed of wild rice and mixed vegetables.

During dinner the two friends laughed and giggled like school girls. Nikki reminisced about law school and some of the characters she had class with everyday. Out of everyone who had taken the Bar so far, only a hand full had actually passed. Bobbi was right about her persevering because it was no easy task studying for the Bar a second time. But law was her passion; and here she was tonight celebrating her accomplishments.

When the waitress returned to the table to check on them, she could see that Bobbi and Nikki were just about done with dinner.

"Would you ladies like dessert?"

When Bobbi looked at her to answer, her eyes were drawn to a couple walking on the other side of the restaurant. She pulled her eyes away from them long enough to say yes. Then she turned her attention back to the couple across the room.

Nikki tried to follow the direction of her stare. "What is it? You see someone you know?"

"Girl, you're not going to believe this. Savon just walked in with his fiancée."

Surprised and excited at the same time Nikki was at full attention now. "No way," she commented. "Where?" Nikki turned in her seat to see if she could pick them out without Bobbi showing her.

"That's him over there in the white shirt; she has on a pink top. You see him?"

Nikki pointed discretely. "You mean him? The finest joker up in here?" Nikki turned back around. "You were right girl, he is fine as hell." Nikki glanced back at him and shook he head. "A man that fine is trouble with a capital T. Money and good looks in a man is nothing but grief I tell you; especially if a woman thinks she can hold him down with the variety of coochie that surely comes his way." Nikki sipped her drink. "You know, all coochie ain't good coochie."

Bobbi stared at Nikki in disbelief. "Girl, what in the world are you talking about? All I did was show you the man and here you are talking about coochie. You need Jesus."

Nikki laughed. "Show you right. That's why I'll be in church tomorrow. You going?"

"If I can get up on time." Bobbi waved her off. "But anyway, back to Savon. I think I'll go over there and say hello before we leave."

"You sure you want to do that? I mean, you don't really know how he'll respond if you only met him that one time, especially since he's here with his fiancée."

"I hear you. But it's all good. If she gives me attitude then I'll forget about the possibility of being friends with him. No harm, no foul."

Even though Nikki agreed with Bobbi, her radar was picking up something different than what her friend was saying. Bobbi had only met Savon once, so what was so different about him that made her want to press the issue of getting to know him, Nikki wondered.

Chapter 18

Nikki was surprised when a group of their friends joined them for dessert. Bobbi had arranged for them to meet her at the restaurant at eight thirty to join in the celebration.

After dessert they moved the party over to the bar area which was more like an upscale meat market. All the unaccompanied men sat and stood around talking, pretending to watch television while the woman pretended to be engaged in meaningful conversation with their girlfriends. Both sexes knew good and well they were checking each other out.

Jokes, laughter and good spirits filled the air. Bobbi couldn't believe how well everything had turned out. Nothing was better than being in the company of good people. And Nikki genuinely seemed to be enjoying her special night.

Bobbi was laughing at one of Nikki's silly comments when her full bladder signaled now or never.

"Hey Nikki, I'm going to the restroom, you coming?"

Nikki turned to face Bobbi. "Nope, I'm good."

"Well hold this for me." She handed Nikki her drink. "Be right back."

The restrooms were half way between the bar area and the dining area. Just as Bobbi turned to walk down the hallway towards the restroom, she looked in the direction of the table were Savon was sitting. *Bingo*. He was alone. Deciding this was her opportunity to go over and speak, she did just that, hoping to be gone before his woman returned.

Savon didn't see her approach because his back was to her.

"So, Mister Turner. How interesting to see you here," Bobbi announced standing behind him.

Savon craned his neck to see who was speaking to him. His eyes grew wide when he saw it was Bobbi. But he recovered quickly.

"How's it going?" she asked. She never moved from her place behind his chair.

Savon turned completely around to face her. "It's Bobbi, right?" he asked with uncertainty.

Bobbi couldn't believe he was acting like he didn't remember her name. Humph.

"Yep, it's Bobbi." She didn't know whether to be mad or what. This joker had damn near talked her ear off on the plane, now he didn't know her name. Amazing. But she wouldn't give him the satisfaction of knowing that she was disappointed.

"You dining alone?" she asked. Of course she already knew the answer, but he didn't know that. She was just making small talk while she figured out her exit strategy.

"Nah. My fiancée is here."

"Oh. Okay." Just then Bobbi looked up and saw Miss Lady walking their way. For shits and grins, Bobbi hung around a bit longer to see how Savon would handle the situation.

The look on his fiancée's face was sheer challenge when she saw Bobbi. Once she reached the table she said hello and sat down. Her delivery was dry.

Savon grabbed her hand. "Babe, this is Bobbi Farqua. She owns a PR Firm."

"Bobbi this is my fiancée, Monica."

"Hello Monica." Bobbi extended her hand.

Monica smiled a half hearted smile. She ignored Bobbi's out stretched hand.

"How do you know her Savon," Monica asked almost accusingly.

"We met a couple of weeks ago on the flight from Atlanta to DC."

Bobbi couldn't believe how Monica was disrespecting her. She was questioning Savon about her like she wasn't even standing there. It was definitely time to bounce.

"Well you two have a good night." With a less than genuine smile, Bobbi nodded towards them and made her way to the restroom.

Chapter 19

July fourth was only a few days away. The biggest buzz around town for the holiday weekend was a pre-season party being thrown at Club Dream for the Washington Warriors by one of their sponsors.

Nikki's cousin Gavin had invited both of them to hang out with him at the event but Bobbi had declined. Initially she thought she might chill with Tony, but he was going out of town for the weekend. So instead of making plans to curl up with a good book Saturday night, she picked up the phone to call Nikki and let her know that she wanted to go to the party.

Nikki picked up on the third ring. "What's up B?

"Hey Nik. I changed my mind about the party this weekend. Do I need to call Gavin to let him know?"

Nikki decided to give Bobbi a hard time. "Oh, so you want to go now, huh? Your change of heart wouldn't have anything to do with a certain gentleman you met on a plane would it?" She knew Bobbi wouldn't like her comment; especially since that night at Indi Blu when Savon sort of played her.

"Of course not, smart ass." Bobbi rolled her eyes. "Forget Savon. I changed my mind because I don't have anything else to do. Plus everyone I know will be there. I figure I may as well use the opportunity to network."

"Calm down, girl. I was just messing with you." Nikki said. "Give Gavin a call on his private cell number. You have it, right?"

"Yep. I got it." Bobbi double checked her Blackberry. "Alrighty then. Let me get off of this phone and get some work done. Talk to you later."

"Okay. Call and let me know what Gavin says. Peace."

Chapter 20

The third floor VIP area in Club Dream was jumping. Every baller shot-caller in the place was on the floor grooving to *Good Life* by *Kanye West*. Even the DJ was pumping his fist from where he stood in the booth.

Bobbi had on dark skinny jeans, a black silk spaghetti strap baby doll sheath, and black four inch peep toe sling-backs. Nikki wore a fitted mid-thigh red dress with gold jewel encrusted three inch sandals.

The two had been at the club for thirty minutes before they ventured up to the third floor. They were beginning to think the event was more of a networking social than the finger snapping shindig they had expected. On the ground level, folks were either hanging around the huge bar which occupied most of the floor, or watching two bald head brothers play pool in a corner. The second floor had small crowds standing around in business suits enveloped in their own private conversations. But when they stepped in the dimly lit open space on level three, they knew this was the place to be. The energy was contagious. All the party animals were there choppin' it up in VIP.

"Ooh. That's my jam," Nikki said waving her hand in the air. "Come on B, let's go dance."

Bobbi looked around and hunched her shoulders. "Okay."

They worked their way through the crowded dance floor and stopped next to a football player they both recognized. He was moving from side to side whispering in his dance partner's ear. Bobbi and Nikki basically squeezed them out of their space since they weren't concerned with dancing all that much any way.

When Bobbi and Nikki were kids, they spent hours in the summertime learning choreography from music videos. Then they would invite their families to a talent show on the weekends to watch them show off their stuff.

Now in VIP, the two friends were dancing together like they were ten-years-old. They did the latest dances and even took a trip down memory lane with some of the old ones like the snake, the whop, the prep, and a few other favorites. But being from the South, they didn't consider a night of dancing complete unless they had a chance to drop-it-like-it's-hot a few times. However, this snooty event didn't lend itself to that kind of fun so they had to keep it dignified.

"There's Gavin," Bobbi said pointing across the room.

"Where?" Nikki turned in the direction Bobbi was pointing. "Oh, I see him. Let's go see what that fool is up to."

"What's up cuz?" Nikki said giving Gavin a hug. He was hands down her favorite cousin. He grew up in Birmingham, Alabama, less than three hours away so they saw each other often and kept in touch when they both went away to college.

"Yo, what's up? You just get here?"

Bobbi stood in the background watching the exchange. "So you don't see anybody else standing here." Her hands were on her hips.

"What's up girl, with yo fine ass." He grabbed her by the arm and pulled her to him. "You look good as hell. Come here and give big daddy some love." Gavin used to have a serious crush on Bobbi when they were kids but she was like family so he never pursued it, even after they grew up. But if she kept looking like she did tonight he might have to change that.

Bobbi rolled her eyes at him. “Shut up boy,” she said laughing and giving him love. Gavin was definitely fine, but he was family so she didn’t think of him otherwise.

Nikki smacked her lips. “Are y’all done with all that incest talk? If so, can a sister get a drink or what?”

Bobbi and Gavin looked at Nikki then at each other and shook their heads. True enough, they all considered each other family, so whenever Gavin and Bobbi carried on with each other romantic like, she would tease them.

“Whatever,” said Bobbi as she reached up and kissed Gavin on the cheek, never taking her eyes off of Nikki.

“Alright…keep it up. Everybody knows kisses lead to sex and then babies. So if y’all keep kissing on each other like that your children’s mom and dad will also be their cousins.”

Bobbi and Gavin looked at each other and frowned.

“Girl, what in the hell are you talking about?” Gavin asked, perplexed.

“Don’t worry about it,” Nikki responded. “Can we get some drinks or what?”

Gavin asked what they wanted and left for the bar.

When he returned with their drinks Bobbi and Nikki moved on to check out the other VIP rooms on the fourth and fifth floor. Just as they made it to the fourth floor, Nikki ran into a friend from undergrad. Bobbi excused herself and continued working her way through the club. As she mingled, she was surprised at how many people she knew from other social events around town.

When she made it to the top floor which was also the rooftop, she went to the bar to freshen up her drink. The fifth floor was by far her favorite. Crisp white sheets suspended as canopies over the seating areas, and dim lighting from torches created an ambiance which made her feel like she had walked into a romantic fantasy.

She walked over to the terrace to check out the view. The warm July air held a gentle breeze. Wispy strands of her hair floated across her face. She closed her eyes and inhaled deeply. The breeze was soothing.

Below, people were still trying to get in. *Good luck*, Bobbi thought. If your name wasn't on the list, it wasn't happening. But she could definitely understand why they kept trying. Club Dream was the place to be tonight; especially if you were into the celebrity scene. To the right of the crowd, there was an attendant posted up at the entrance to the parking lot which resembled a high-end showroom. There were Benzes, Bimmer's, Range Rovers, sports cars; you name it, it was out there.

Humming along to the music in the background, Bobbi took a sip of her drink. As she moved the glass away from her lips she felt a soft tap on her shoulder. She turned around.

"Bobbi. How are you?" Savon said in a low voice. His hands were in his jean pockets.

Humph. Now he remembers my name. Amazing. Bobbi's response didn't reflect her thoughts.

"Hello Savon. I'm well. How are you?" Her smile was genuine but guarded. Surely he wasn't here alone, and she wasn't in the mood to rise above Monica's jealousy and snide remarks tonight. She wouldn't make a scene, but she would definitely make it clear to Monica that fucking with her was a bad move.

“Chillin’,” he responded.

“I see.” Bobbi nodded her head. She wasn’t going to take the lead with this conversation or make Savon feel comfortable with her. She wasn’t so sure he was the cool homeboy she met on the plane any way. Maybe that meeting was a fluke and the real Savon had showed himself at Indi Blu.

Savon didn’t know what to say to Bobbi since he had played her at the restaurant. So why didn’t he just continue to admire her from afar? His eyes had been all over her since she stepped foot onto the fifth floor. And so were every other man’s in VIP. She hadn’t noticed him but the way her jeans fit her perfectly round ass had him at full attention.

Savon shifted on his feet. “Look, Bobbi. I owe you an apology for how things went down at the restaurant a couple of weeks ago. Monica can be a little jealous at times. But she didn’t mean anything by it.”

Bobbi stared up at Savon for a moment. She wasn’t sure if she should respond to his weak excuse or not. It was his behavior that had thrown her off balance, not Monica’s.

“Personally, I thought the whole episode was a bit much, but you don’t have to apologize to me for Monica’s behavior. It is what it is.”

“So we’re good,” he asked relieved she wasn’t mad.

“Of course.” Bobbi was finished with this conversation. She took a small sip of her martini. “Well it was good seeing you again, Savon.” Smiling, she dismissed him. “Take care.” She stepped past him and went to look for Nikki.

Chapter 21

It was early August and only days away from the Washington Warriors first pre-season game. However, Savon was finding it increasingly difficult to stay focused. Monica hadn't stopped badgering him with comments about Bobbi since he introduced them two months ago. Although he really loved Monica, it was a blessing in disguise that she had remained in Atlanta after he was traded and moved to DC.

Being a professional model afforded Monica the luxury of staying with Savon for long visits between projects. But her frequent visits throughout the summer had already proven to be challenging, especially when she had jealous fits. Nevertheless, the issue with Bobbi was a small problem compared to the troubles that dropped on his plate last week.

Now this chic LaShawn had him worried about a paternity situation. LaShawn had been blowing up his cell talking about he was the father of her two-year-old son. Savon didn't know how long he could keep this from Monica, or hold off LaShawn from going to the media with her story. LaShawn was determined to pin him down as the father and refused to listen to reason. Regretfully, he knew exactly who she was and the mistake he made. But there was no way he had fathered a child with her.

Pressures were already mounting for him to perform and meet the expectations of his new team and coaches. And now he had to deal with a false claim of paternity. No doubt, Monica would burst a blood vessel when she found out. The only question was should he tell her now or let her find out publicly like everyone else.

When the calls kept coming from LaShawn, and finally her attorney, Savon realized this crazy lie wouldn't go away quietly. He thought about calling his attorney for guidance but decided he would much rather mull over the situation with someone he trusted first. The only person he could think of who would have both relevant professional advice as well as an objective personal opinion was Bobbi.

Sure, they weren't friends but something about her was trustworthy. And he knew she was a straight forward person even with their limited interaction. So he retrieved her business card from his wallet and dialed her work number.

"Good morning. My Way Communications, this is Cierra. How may I help you?"

"Good morning. My name is Savon Turner; I'm calling for Bobbi Farqua."

"I'm sorry Mr. Turner," said the perky young assistant. "Miss Farqua is unavailable at the moment. Is there a message?"

"Sure." Savon left his number and a short message for Bobbi to return his call as soon as she could; that it was urgent he speak with her. Cierra made a note of the information and ended the call.

"Good morning Miss Farqua," Cierra's cheerful voice rang as Bobbi entered the office. She wore black framed glasses and a clip on ponytail in the crown of her head. When she smiled her dimples went deep like tiny pockets.

"Good morning Cierra. How are you today?" Bobbi asked as she looked through the messages on the counter in front of Cierra's desk.

"I'm fine. Oh, that message is from Mr. Turner. He called at nine and said it was urgent that he speak with you.

Humph. Bobbi took the messages and went to her office. She couldn't image what Savon needed to talk to her about; urgently at that.

She looked up at the wall clock across from her desk—it was ten thirty. If Savon wanted to talk to her, now would be the best time so she dialed the number on the message.

When Savon answered, he thanked Bobbi for returning his call then asked if he could meet with her in her office. The most he would say over the telephone was that something important had come up and that he needed her professional advice. Her curiosity was piqued but she didn't ask any questions. She checked her schedule. There was no way she could see him today unless he came during her lunch time which she usually reserved for returning calls and responding to e-mails. But from the intensity in his voice, she knew whatever he wanted to talk about was serious.

"Can you be here by noon?" Bobbi inquired.

"Yes. I'll be there," he said with a sigh of relief.

"Okay. The address is on my card which I assume you have since you called."

"Yes, I have the address. See you at twelve."

Savon hung up the phone feeling like he had made the right decision by calling Bobbi. She was level headed and smart—exactly what he needed to figure this thing out. But the biggest challenge yet was finding a way to tell Monica.

Chapter 22

Cierra's eyes grew as big as silver dollars when Savon walked into the office. It was one thing to see athletes on television but it was quite another to see them in living color.

She cleared her throat. "May I help you?"

"Yes. I'm Savon Turner, here to see Miss Farqua."

"Oh, yes. She's expecting you. Have a seat...she'll be right out." As soon as Savon turned his back to walk to the sitting area, Cierra peered over the counter to get a better look at him. She fanned herself. *Mercy!*

Cierra called Bobbi. "Miss Farqua, Mr. Turner is here to see you."

"Great. Can you bring him back? I'm on another call."

"Sure thing," Cierra replied. She hung up the phone and walked around her desk to escort Savon to Bobbi's office.

Bobbi motioned for Savon to have a seat in front of her desk. She covered the mouthpiece with her hand and whispered thank you to Cierra. Seconds later she ended her call.

"Hello Savon. I'm almost afraid to ask how it's going," Bobbi commented.

"Hey Bobbi."

"Before we go any further, would you like some water?"

"Yes, thanks."

Bobbi stood in her charcoal gray pant suit and walked over to the small refrigerator in the corner of her feminine but professional office. The space wasn't very big, but there was enough room for her desk, a couple of chairs, a loveseat, two file cabinets, a huge bookshelf and the refrigerator. The office was decorated in chocolate brown and lime green with splashes of brighter colors.

"So tell me what's going on." She handed him a bottled water and returned to her desk.

Savon told her about LaShawn and the phone calls he'd been receiving for the last three weeks. He told her how the first call from LaShawn was more of an invitation for the two of them to hang out and get reacquainted. But when he told her that he wasn't interested and that he had a fiancée she flipped out and the calls became demanding and harassing. Then Savon hesitated before revealing the full weight of why he wanted to consult with Bobbi.

"LaShawn said I'm the father of her two-year-old son." Once he got it out he made full eye contact with Bobbi. Her expression was intense but neutral. He couldn't tell what she was thinking.

"Well, is he yours?" she asked matter-of-factly. Her full attention focused on his body language and his eyes, looking for any indication that he was lying.

"Absolutely not. But LaShawn is adamant that he is. She even had her attorney call me on Friday basically threatening me to take responsibility or they would see me in court."

"Three questions for you Savon. One and two: Did you have sex with her? And if so, how can you be so sure the child isn't yours? And three: why are you asking for my advice? Don't you have an attorney?

"To answer your first two questions, yes, I had sex with her but I used protection. And to answer your third question, yes, I have an attorney whom I plan to call after I finish speaking with you. The problem is I don't have a publicist any more. That's why I wanted your opinion."

Bobbi didn't waste any time giving Savon what he came for—her opinion. She told him that he should take everything LaShawn and her attorney said very seriously even if he was certain the child wasn't his.

"Do you think she'll go public with this?" Bobbi gulped down some water.

"Yeah, I think so." Savon took a deep breath. "At least that's what she said last week right before I got the call from her attorney."

"Well if that's true, I recommend you hire a publicist to represent you in case this becomes media frenzy."

Savon didn't know how Bobbi would feel about him as a client but he liked the way she handled business. She was thorough and he wanted her on his team. When he asked if she would consider signing him on as a client, she didn't respond right away. Instead, she suggested that he get in touch with his attorney, bring him up to speed then give her a call.

Chapter 23

Savon left Bobbi's office and headed straight for his attorney, Raymond Mayfield. After Savon unloaded the entire story on him, Mayfield wanted to contact LaShawn's attorney before things got any worse. But unfortunately they were too late.

Bobbi called Savon on his cell phone to see if he was watching CNN. When he said no, she suggested he find a television with the quickness. LaShawn had chosen today to go public with her story. It was national news now.

Damn! Monica. Savon hoped it wouldn't come to this—at least not until he had a chance to sit down with Monica and explain himself.

Savon still had Bobbi on the line when he motioned for a stately Mayfield with salt and pepper hair to follow him out to the lobby. There was a television mounted on the wall in the waiting area. Savon heard the voices on the news channel before he saw the screen. LaShawn was at a press conference with the two-year-old boy and her attorney lying through her teeth about how he wasn't taking care of his son.

Mayfield asked Savon for his phone so he could talk to Bobbi. He asked if she could come over right away so the three of them could talk things through and determine their next move. They needed to be unified in their approach and how they were going to handle the media.

After Bobbi told Mayfield she could be there by five, he said goodbye and handed the phone back to Savon. But Bobbi had already hung up.

"So what's the deal," Savon asked Attorney Mayfield.

"Bobbi agreed to meet us here in my office at five." He looked at his watch. "And since that's not for two hours, I suggest you get out of here and find your fiancée so you can do damage control. Consider bringing her back here with you this evening. It may help smooth things over. At the very least she'll get to hear the facts and know first hand how we plan to handle the situation. But that's your call to make. See you at five."

Attorney Mayfield left Savon standing in the lobby.

Oh boy. Bobbi released a deep sigh and slumped down in her chair. How did she get herself into this one? Savon had blind-sided her with this big bag of dirty laundry and now expected her help. And although she wanted to do whatever she could for him, she couldn't help but think that his jealous nut basket woman would have a problem with it. To make matters worse, seeing him today was a reminder of just how attracted Bobbi was to him.

In two hours she would be meeting with Savon and his attorney to strategize and counter what LaShawn said at the press conference. Bobbi needed to make sure Cierra was on board with the adjustments they needed to make in her schedule today in order for her to prepare for the meeting.

Bobbi called Cierra into her office. "Cierra, I need you to reschedule my last two appointments today. See if we can fit them in on Wednesday. Mr. Turner has decided to sign on with us so I need to get a contract ready to take with me to the meeting at his attorney's office."

"Yes, ma'am. Do you need help with the contract?"

"No, I can handle it. But I will need you to hold all of my calls for the rest of the day so I can get out of here by four."

"Okee dokee." She started out the door then turned on her heels to look at Bobbi. "You think it's his kid?

"I really don't know." Bobbi looked up from her work. "But a paternity test and about two weeks will tell."

Chapter 24

In Attorney Mayfield's office they got down to business. He had already spoken with LaShawn's attorney so he was prepared to advise Savon and Bobbi of their next step when they arrived. For the record, Savon told his story again blow by blow, leaving nothing out.

He paced the floor while Bobbi and Mayfield sat and listened as he revealed the details of his encounter with LaShawn.

"It happened here in DC at an away game when I played for the Atlanta Condors. After the game I returned to the hotel with the rest of the team and a few of us went downstairs to the bar to celebrate our win. That's when I met LaShawn. She was there with her friends so we all hung out at the hotel bar drinking, partying and talking shit. As things go, the bar closed, one thing led to the next and LaShawn and I ended up in my hotel room going at it hot and heavy. I'll admit, that Grey Goose had me feeling real nice but I wasn't so wasted that I forgot to strap up before we had sex. Maybe LaShawn was too gone to realize I put on a condom, but I did. But the reason I know for a fact that I can't be the father of her son is that she literally passed out or feel asleep—one of the two –before I had a chance to climax so I pulled out." Savon wiped his face with his hand and continued. "That whole scene kind of messed me up. Not knowing what else to do, I checked her pulse—relieved that she still had one—

I left her sleeping on the bed and carried all of my things with me to my boy's room down the hall."

"Wow," was all Bobbi could say. For once she was speechless.

"Well, Savon," Attorney Mayfield interjected. "After speaking with LaShawn's attorney, I ordered a paternity test for both you and her son. You can go to the lab tomorrow."

After listening to Savon's account of what happened and considering the extent of his relationship with LaShawn, Bobbi was ready to go to work for her client. Even though the story was a bit bizarre, she believed him. Anything was possible with alcohol in the mix. She patted the seat next to her and asked Savon to sit down. She went over the contract with him to make their verbal agreement official.

Attorney Mayfield excused himself while they handled business. Bobbi explained the services she offered for this particular situation as well as how she could support his career and reputation long term. While she waited for Savon to read through both contracts, she took the opportunity to draft a statement for his approval.

Before the meeting, Savon had told Mayfield and Bobbi that the media had already started calling him for comment. So first thing tomorrow morning Bobbi would send out a press release. At this point, she felt making a personal appearance was premature and unnecessary. They would hold off on an actual press conference with the media until they received the paternity test results.

Savon looked at Bobbi. "You have a pen? I'm ready to sign."

"Here." Bobbi gave him the pen she was writing with. "So are you a temporary client or does My Way Communications have your business for the foreseeable future?" she asked with a smile.

He chuckled. "You couldn't get rid of me if you wanted to."

"Alrighty then," she teased. "Check this out." She showed him a draft of the release she planned to send out tomorrow.

Mr. Turner has requested a paternity test and is confident this misunderstanding will be cleared up shortly. He asks that the media respect his privacy until the results are back. Thank you.

"That's what's up," Savon said nodding his approval. "So you say you'll send it out tomorrow morning?"

She smiled at him. "Shall I take that as an approval to move forward?"

"Yes! I wish you could send it out tonight."

Bobbi chuckled. "Tomorrow will be soon enough."

Now that Savon had a trusted team working on his behalf to clear up this mess, he could focus on the hardest part of this whole scandal: facing Monica.

Chapter 25

"So you finally decided to come home, huh?" Monica swung the door open nearly pulling it off the hinges when she heard Savon put his key in the door. She was livid.

"Monica, I told you I had to meet with my attorney and publicist. If you didn't trust me, you should have come with me," he said in a much calmer tone than hers. He stepped inside and tossed his keys on the table in the foyer.

"Trust? What the fuck could you possibly know about trust? Huh? Here I am walking around on your arm, wearing your ring, and you're out there sleeping around making babies. Don't talk to me about trust," she screamed at the top of her lungs. She followed him into the family room.

Savon released a heavy sigh and sat on the sofa. "Look Monica, I'm sorry this happened. But I told you already, it's not my kid. Why can't you try to understand and support me on this?"

Monica stood in front of Savon looking down at him. He had some nerve asking her to support his cheating ass. "So, let me get this straight," she said with much attitude. "You couldn't keep your dick in your pants, and I need to understand that? That hooker's public accusations put me under the spotlight just like they did you. But I'm the one looking like a fool while you shine." Monica was getting more pissed off with every word she said. Smoke rings floated out of her ears. "You know what? I'm out of here." She stormed off towards the staircase.

Savon jumped up off the sofa and went after her. He grabbed her arm before she made it to the first step. "Monica, that was three years ago. You and I were just dating at the time so why are you tripping?"

"Whatever, Savon." She snatched her arm away and climbed the stairs. Within an hour she was out the door.

Bobbi was mentally exhausted by the time she got home. The first thing she did was take a hot shower and put on her favorite red silk robe from Korea with the colorful embossed dragon on the back. She purchased it on a trip to the country while she was in the military. And five years later with at least five others in her closet it was still her first choice.

In the kitchen she prepared a salad of mixed greens, olives, red onions, cranberries and walnuts. She topped it off with a Mango Vinaigrette and grabbed a bottle of water from the refrigerator. After dinner she went back upstairs to her bedroom to review some papers for work and to check her phone messages. As expected, she had a call from Nikki asking if she'd heard about Savon. She also had messages from her mom and Tony.

Usually her mom was in bed by nine so she called her first. It had been a week since they talked so she definitely needed to catch up with her to see how she was doing. She called Tony next. Although she had spoken with him a number of times since she returned from Atlanta two months ago, she had only seen him twice. They laughed and talked, teasing each other until they were both hot and bothered. So they planned a midnight rendezvous for Friday night. Before they hung up, Tony asked Bobbi to accompany him to a company party in two weeks.

Nikki answered on the first ring. She couldn't wait to hear what, if anything, Bobbi knew about Savon's paternity scandal. This was Savon's first season playing in Washington so Gavin and the other Warriors players she talked to didn't know anything about his personal business.

"Give it up Miss PR. I know you got the 4-1-1 on ya' boy," Nikki prodded with excitement.

"Oh, I'm fine. Thanks for asking," Bobbi commented.

Nikki smacked her lips. "I don't have time for that right now. What I want to know is what's up with Savon and I know you know something."

"And you would be correct. As of six o'clock this evening Savon is now my client."

Nikki's jaw dropped and she covered her mouth with her hand. "Seriously?" Fate was something else, Nikki thought. "How did that happen?"

Bobbi ran the story down for Nikki, starting with Savon's call to her office that morning. She gave her every detail up until the meeting at his attorney's office. The actual account of events Savon shared during their meeting with Attorney Mayfield would remain in her confidence because of her ethical obligation to her client. If Savon decided to go public with his story after the press conference she hoped to have in a week or so, that would be his choice. Until then, if the rumor mill was fed it wouldn't be on her watch.

Chapter 26

Back in Atlanta, Monica refused to take any of Savon's calls. He didn't know what to think about their relationship or how to handle the situation. On top of that, all the rumors circulating—the questioning looks of his coaches and teammates, and the intrusive media bugging him to death—were getting the best of him. He really needed someone to talk to. Someone who wouldn't judge him or take what he said and use it for their own gain; just one person he could trust. He decided that person was Bobbi.

After Monica left, he visited Bobbi's office every day that week. More than anything he needed the comfort of being around someone who believed in him and his story.

To his dismay, LaShawn was procrastinating with taking her son for his paternity test. So as time passed and he waited for the results he and Bobbi spent a lot of time together, especially in her office. Cierra had blocked out an hour on Bobbi's schedule every day for him. And whenever their schedules permitted, they would meet for dinner and just hang out.

Bobbi enjoyed their conversations and spending time with him. Savon was so easy to talk to and they just clicked in a way that was refreshing. For the first time in years her relationship with a man wasn't based on sex and keeping the upper hand. Rather, their connection was based on character and merit. It was strange; sometimes when she was around him she thought for sure her heart fluttered.

However, the times he talked about his relationship woes with Monica, she could see how broken up he was about her leaving. Those were the moments that snapped Bobbi back to reality. Savon was a man in love; hurting because his woman left him to no fault of his own—at least not in his mind. So Bobbi would listen to what he had to say and reassure him that things would work out. But she always stopped short of giving him advice.

One night after dinner when they were about to get in their separate cars, Savon walked up on her. He stood so close that Bobbi could feel his breath as he talked.

"Bobbi. Thanks for listening to me and believing in me." His words were tenderly spoken.

She looked up at him. "I appreciate your honesty, Savon, and being real about what went down. It makes what I do worthwhile to help vindicate someone unfairly accused."

He was intense, and she felt uncomfortable. Her immediate reaction was to say something silly to lighten the mood but he closed the small distance between them and embraced her. He smelled so good; crisp and masculine, and he felt even better. Bobbi thought she would melt right there in his arms.

He kissed her on the forehead and stepped back. "Thanks, again Bobbi—for everything," he said then opened her car door.

"You're welcome," was all she said. When she got in the car and he closed the door, she cranked up and pulled off. When she checked her rearview mirror, he was standing next to his black chromed out Escalade with blacked out windows, watching her disappear into the night.

Chapter 27

Finally, the DNA results were back. Attorney Mayfield had called on a few favors to get the results and they just happened to come in on Labor Day. They had all been waiting far too long to have this escapade drag out any longer. He called Bobbi to give her the news before he called Savon.

"Yes!" Bobbi shouted into the phone. "Whew. I wasn't holding my breath or anything like that but it sure is good to hear that he's in the clear. If it's okay with you, can I give Savon the news?"

"No problem, Bobbi. Make sure you tell him to call me right away so we can move forward with his case. Then the three of us can meet tomorrow to get the ball rolling."

"Will do, Attorney Mayfield. I'm on my way over to give him the news as soon as I hang up with you."

Bobbi jumped in the shower, threw on a denim mini skirt and a tank top, and slid her feet into a pair of wedged heel slides. She pulled her hair into a ponytail, applied eye-liner and mascara, and smoothed on a little pink lip gloss. Within thirty minutes she was out the door on her way to Savon's house.

About half way there she decided it was best to call ahead and make sure he was home. After all, it was only ten A.M. She told him that she needed to talk about something concerning the case and asked if it was okay for her to stop by. Savon wondered what was so important that she needed to come by his house; especially since she had never been over before. Nonetheless, he told her it was no problem, and that he would be waiting.

Although Bobbi hadn't been to Savon's house before, she knew where he lived. One evening after they had dinner, he drove past with her in tow to show off his new home purchase. That's when she realized he lived in the same neighborhood as another of her acquaintances so she new exactly where she was going.

Fifteen minutes after calling Savon, she pulled into his circular driveway. She checked herself in the rearview mirror. She was cheesing so hard her cheeks were hurting. Satisfied with her looks, she made her way to the front door. He opened it just as she rang the bell.

"Miss Farqua. To what do I owe this nice surprise?" He was genuinely pleased to see her.

Bobbi didn't know whether to melt or talk. "Hi, Savon. I have something to tell you." She was giddy.

"Come on in," he said and stepped aside.

Bobbi followed him to the family room but she didn't take a seat when he offered. Instead she told him that she needed to stand for what she had to say. For a brief moment she just stared at him smiling. Then she began to speak.

"In the words of *Maury Povich*: Savon Turner you are NOT the father."

It took a few seconds for Bobbi's words to register. But when they did, Savon was hyped.

"Are you serious?" he asked with both hands on his head. He couldn't believe it. "It's finally over? Four weeks of pure hell. It's finally over!"

Before either of them knew what was happening Savon had scooped Bobbi up off her feet and was spinning her around in circles. Caught up in the moment, they both laughed—her from excitement, and him from happiness and relief.

When the reality of their closeness hit them, Savon stopped in his tracks. Bobbi was still in his arms, her feet dangling at least a foot above the floor. They were at eye level, only nose length apart.

"Uhhh...I think you should put me down now," Bobbi said feeling awkward.

Savon didn't say a word, but rather loosened his grip on her just enough for her body to slide slowly down the length of his. When her feet touched the floor their eyes were still locked and her arms were still wrapped around his neck.

There was silence. The next thing Bobbi knew, his lips were on hers; tender at first then hungry like he needed more. His passion was mind numbing. She reached for his face to deepen the kiss and his hands dropped to her lower back. Seconds later, Savon's ringing telephone brought them back to reality. They slowly released each other.

She hoped he would, but figured he wasn't going to answer the phone by the third ring. His piercing stare was burning a whole in the top of her head but she refused to look into his eyes. Suddenly, brushing imaginary lint from her tank top became the focus of her attention. This scene was just too intense for her; she had to get out of there.

She cleared her throat. "I think I should go."

He brushed his index finger across her cheek. "Okay." He walked her to the door.

Bobbi took a deep breath to regain her composure. "I almost

forgot to tell you. Mayfield wants you to call him right away. He also said the three of us need to meet tomorrow to coordinate our next move." She looked at him with genuine sincerity.

"Congratulations, Savon."

"Thanks for coming by to give me the news," he said.

Bobbi smiled and got out of there as quickly as she could without looking like a lunatic. She was definitely shaken by their kiss and hoped it wasn't obvious to Savon.

Chapter 28

Bobbi was frantic on her ride home. How could she let this happen? Seriously though, kissing Savon was taboo on so many levels. First, and most importantly was the fact that he was almost married, which meant complications and eventual drama with a capital D. And she had already had a taste of what Monica was like. Things would definitely end in a man-down situation—meaning someone would get seriously hurt.

Second, her libido had been in overdrive since they started spending time together over the last four weeks. Although she had Tony and a few others in her back pocket if she wanted to get her groove on, after that kiss, the only one who could squelch what was brewing in the pit of her stomach was Savon.

And lastly, but most concerning was how she felt when she was with him. Life had taught her a long time ago that emotions were not dependable when it came to men. In fact they could even be dangerous. That's why she lived her life the way she did. But she couldn't deny the lightness of her heart when Savon kissed her.

After exiting his subdivision, Bobbi pulled into traffic and drove a mile before stopping at a red light—her thoughts still on that life altering kiss. Her heart was racing; her body tingling. She found it hard to focus on anything else, including driving.

What in the hell is wrong with me? You would think I've never kissed a man before. But that kiss....

Bobbi exhaled. She had wanted Savon since the first day she laid eyes on him. But not in a million years would she have thought kissing him could be better than her fantasies. Not with her vivid imagination.

When the light turned green, Bobbi lost all sensibility. *I have to know what would have happened if I hadn't left.* She swung a u-turn at the next intersection and high-tailed it back to Savon's. When she knocked on the door, she freed her mind of all the reasons why she shouldn't be there. This was her window of opportunity.

Savon opened the door and smiled at Bobbi. No words were spoken. He reached for her hand and pulled her inside. She started to say something but he shook his head and put a finger on her lips to hush her. His lips replaced his finger. And eventually his lips replaced all of her clothes.

Savon took Bobbi upstairs to his bed and spent the rest of the day pleasing her. There wasn't a dry spot on her body by the time he was finished. Whenever she tried to reciprocate the favor he would shake his head and give her even more pleasure. He only stopped working her over long enough to feed her, and then went straight back to it. At times, if she didn't know better, Bobbi felt certain he was making love to her.

When Bobbi pulled into her driveway it was midnight. She headed straight for the kitchen to try and replenish what she'd lost through sweat and exertion. There was no doubt in her mind that her electrolytes and sodium count were dangerously low.

She laughed. Savon was the T-R-U-T-H. They did things to each other she was embarrassed to remember, let alone tell someone. A chill went up her spine and her shoulders shimmied at the thought.

Bobbi carried a tray of cheese, crackers and strawberries up to her room. She popped a strawberry in her mouth and went to take a shower. Undressing, she caught a glimpse of herself smiling in the mirror. Why was she so giddy? He's just a man, and it was just sex she told herself. *Get yourself together girl.*

Twenty minutes later she lay across her bed refreshed, thinking about the last thirteen hours. What now? As a rule men had to fit into her world—a world that lacked real intimacy. Yet with Savon she felt her heart giving way to something. Exactly what, she didn't know.

She exhaled and shifted to look at the clock on her nightstand. The red digital numbers made her cringe—it was one thirty. She yawned. It was definitely time to get some shut eye. But before she did, she dropped to her knees on the side of her bed to pray.

God, thank you for my life and all of my blessings. Thank you for my family and friends, and for keeping us all safe. God, I feel off balance right now. I've managed to keep my heart hidden from men for a very long time now. But I think someone may have found a way in. Please guide me Lord. I don't want to get in too deep. I love you with all I am. In Jesus' name. Amen.

Chapter 29

Bobbi met Savon at Attorney Mayfield's office early the next morning. When they saw each other, it was business as usual. Bobbi had been a little nervous about seeing him after the wicked things they did to each other yesterday. But Savon was cool. He wasn't weird about anything and actually treated her like he had before he saw her with her clothes off.

So Bobbi, Mayfield, and Savon all agreed that it was time to have a press conference. It was time for the world to know that Savon wasn't guilty of anything more than choosing the wrong woman to lie down with. They scheduled a press conference for two o'clock that same day.

During the press conference, Savon told reporters that the paternity results were conclusive; he was not the father of LaShawn's two-year-old son. When they asked for the real story that led to LaShawn's fraudulent accusations, he took the high road saying that it was water under the bridge now. That all he wanted to do was move forward with his life and the football season. He figured there was no point in revealing the details of the story since nothing he could say would damage LaShawn's character more than she already had.

After the press conference, Bobbi went back to her office to check on things. It was five o'clock and Cierra had already left for the day. She checked her messages and reviewed her schedule for the following day.

With every thing in check, she relaxed, leaning back in her executive chair. Her eyes closed. This had been an incredibly taxing day mentally. She breathed a deep sigh and rubbed the back of her neck. Thank goodness Savon hadn't been weird about them today. Although she could have handled it whichever way he decided to play it, she was relieved that he was the same man she had grown to know before their sexual encounter.

Bobbi didn't realize she had fallen asleep until her ringing Blackberry startled her.

"Hello."

"What are you doing?" Savon asked in a deep sexy voice.

"Hey, Savon. I was just about to leave work. What's up?"

"Can I take you to dinner to celebrate?"

She paused. "I'm a little tired tonight. Can I take a rain check for tomorrow?" She thought maybe she had had enough of Mister Wonderful for one day.

"Come on Bobbi. You can rest after I leave. I really want to show my appreciation for all you did for me. After tonight I'll be on the road for the next two weeks. Don't make me beg because I will if I have to," he teased.

She smiled. Thank God he couldn't see how big she was cheesing. "Hmmm. I might like hearing you beg. What would you say?"

"Oh so you got jokes, huh?" He decided to give her a teaser. "Well, my feelings would be extremely hurt if you didn't accept my invitation. You have been here for me from day one of this madness. And you've even listened to me rattle on about my personal problems. So please, do me the honor of celebrating our victory with me tonight."

Her body tingled. "That was pretty good. How can I turn down an invitation like that?"

Bobbi gave Savon directions to her house and told him she would be ready by eight thirty.

At eight fifteen, Bobbi was putting the finishing touches on her look. She was stunning. She wore a black v-neck dress with Kimono sleeves that stopped right above her knees, and black peep toe pumps. A round platinum pendant hung just above her cleavage. Her hair was straight with a center part. As usual, her make-up was flawless.

When Savon knocked on the door, he wasn't ready for the sexy vixen standing before him. His eyes narrowed to slits as he checked her out from head to toe, nodding his approval. "Nice—very nice."

"Thank you. I'm ready," she sang, loving the reaction she inspired in him. "Just let me grab my purse and keys." She left the door ajar, picked up her things off the table near the door and joined him.

Savon walked around to the passenger side of his Escalade and opened the door for her. She climbed in and got comfortable. This was her first time in his ride. She watched him walk around the front of the truck to get in. He had to be the most attractive man she'd ever met. However, her attraction for him was deeper than just his good looks. He'd proven to be honest, fun, a great conversationalist, and he knew how to treat her, which turned her on beyond her comprehension.

Before he pulled off, he flipped through his CDs asking Bobbi what she wanted to hear. Honestly, it really didn't matter to her whether music played or not because the ensuing battle within her over what was happening between the two of them would drown it out anyway.

Bobbi was fully aware that this wasn't long term or even a situation where she would deal with him like she did her other lovers. What happened between them over the weekend was a one time thing and that was it. He was practically a married man.

Finally, with much indecision they agreed to listen to slow jams on the radio. He cranked up, put the trunk in drive and noticed Bobbi smiling at him.

"What?"

"You smell nice." She could hardly take it; he was overwhelming her senses in so many ways. She knew her comment was corny but she couldn't very well tell him how fine he was and maintain her usual self controlled demeanor. Besides this wasn't even her man, she kept reminding herself.

"Thanks," he replied with a smile to match hers. He drove off.

Chapter 30

Savon made reservations at an exclusive DC restaurant where the list was always booked solid. Even with a two week notice it was tough to get in. Bobbi wondered how he managed to pull it off within a matter of hours.

As they walked into the restaurant, Savon's hand rested in the small of her back. She didn't know how much more of his displays of intimate familiarity she would be able to handle without responding. *Goodness!* He was really testing *her* respect for his engagement. If he didn't start behaving like a man with a fiancée she wouldn't be responsible for her actions.

The hostess checked for their reservation and immediately escorted them to a table near a grand piano in a dimly lit corner. Savon pulled out her seat; made sure she was comfortable then took his.

Their server brought a wine list and menus, filled their water glasses and waited for their drink order. The two decided on a bottle of Merlot to start the evening.

Half a dozen beautiful crystal chandeliers hung from the ceiling, creating a romantic ambiance. Exactly the type of setting she should be avoiding with Savon. But the thing was…this joker didn't seem the least bit phased by it. Actually he appeared to be quite comfortable. Matter of fact, everything about him from the way he was looking at her to the tone in his voice, was laced with seduction.

Dinner was absolutely lovely. Savon even fed her from his plate which sealed the deal for her—she would roll with him despite his situation. As long as he catered to her like he did now, he would be her top pick. To hell with Monica.

It was eleven thirty by the time Savon pulled into Bobbi's driveway. They both had to get up early tomorrow but neither was ready to end the night so she invited him in. Once inside she led him to her entertainment room where she spent time with family and friends when they visited.

"Can I get you something to drink," she offered.

"I'll take water," he replied, and sat on the red leather sectional sofa.

The sexual tension was mounting between them. When she returned with their drinks, Savon took his from her hand and asked her to sit next to him. When she did, he brushed a soft kiss to her lips then whispered in her ear "I want you."

Hearing him say that was the equivalent of opening the flood gates for Bobbi. Her body responded to him like he owned it. For the next hour they made love right there on the sofa, but this time he allowed her to show him what naughty things she wanted to do to his body.

On his ride home, Savon couldn't get Bobbi out of his head. She was everything he wanted in a woman. She was smart, sexy, and beautiful. And she actually listened more than she talked. "Mmm-umph! That woman is addictive," he said aloud.

He hadn't meant to kiss her that first time when she stopped by his house, but he got caught up in the moment and obviously so did she. And when she came back after leaving, it was confirmation that she wanted him as much as he wanted her. The last month had been torture being around her everyday, inhaling her sweet scent and watching her lips move whenever she talked—it was literally driving him crazy.

He parked his truck in the garage when he made it home and went inside. The first thing he did was check his messages—still no call from Monica. It had been frustrating trying to get her to talk to him since she left four weeks ago. The most she talked to him was last week when she told him that she needed her space and time to think.

Even so, he expected to hear something from her since he left a message on her cell phone about the paternity results. For real, if she didn't start acting like his fiancée real soon he was going to call the whole thing off. There is no way he was going to marry her if this was how she was going to treat him whenever a problem surfaced in their relationship.

Savon pulled his luggage out and started packing for his trip. His thoughts naturally turned to Bobbi. He was somewhat confused that she hadn't tripped about them hooking up, but grateful at the same time. Even though she new about Monica leaving, and that things were shaky in their relationship right now, he still half expected her to question him about something. That's just what women do, especially since they wear their feelings on their sleeves.

Savon fell backwards on the bed after he put the last item in his suitcase. Lying on his back, he stared up at the ceiling. Maybe these timely away football games would create the necessary distance to give him time to cool his heels and chill out on the Bobbi situation. He couldn't lie—it was like he craved her even when they were apart. Damn. He didn't know how this would play out but he hoped it wouldn't get ugly. He liked her too much and wanted her to be a permanent fixture in his life even if it meant they could only be friends.

Chapter 31

The next morning, Bobbi called Nikki when she got to work. Nikki had left a message on her work phone as well as her Blackberry inquiring about Savon after seeing the press conference. So much had happened over the last forty-eight hours that this was her first opportunity to call Nikki back.

"Well damn. Good thing a sistah wasn't in jail or needed a ride to the emergency room or something, cause I would've been short," Nikki said. "I called you like three days ago."

"Calm down and stop lying. You called me yesterday, not three days ago."

"Whatever." Nikki chuckled. "So what's up? Savon is not the father, huh?"

"Nope. He was telling the truth all along."

"Interesting." Nikki paused, and then continued. "I don't know LaShawn, but from what I hear she's a professional groupie, always hanging out on the athlete scene."

"Well she picked the wrong one this time. I bet when she went public with her story she never expected it to end like this. I don't know if he'll ever go public with his side of the story but he really doesn't have to. It's a wrap for her."

"For sure—she's done. Anyway, what's been up with you?"

Bobbi didn't mention her romantic involvement with Savon.

She wanted to wait until she was face-to-face with Nikki to drop that bomb.

"What are you doing this weekend," Bobbi asked dismissing Nikki's question.

"I'm working this weekend. Why what's up?"

"I need to talk to you about something in person. How about next weekend?

"I won't be here. I'm going home, remember? Mom is catering a wedding next Saturday and she needs help preparing the food."

Bobbi gave some thought to going home with Nikki. "Maybe I should fly home with you to help out. We might even have time to go shopping or hang out for a while."

"Yeah, you should do that. Mom will be ecstatic. We can hang out when we get there because mom won't be home until after five. So go ahead and get your ticket." Before they hung up, Nikki gave Bobbi her flight arrangements.

Bobbi and Nikki landed in Hot-lanta at noon on Friday. Even though it was mid September the humidity was suffocating. As soon as they stepped outside they both remembered why they lived farther North. Nikki picked up a rental car, blasted the AC and they were on their way to the mall. Later, they would be knee deep in hors d'oeuvres and decorations.

Once Nikki pulled onto the interstate they both called their families to let them know they were in town and would be home by five. Whenever they came home together the two families would have an impromptu reunion, which meant they would be surrounded by family the entire weekend.

Being at home together was like old times for Bobbi and Nikki. They talked so much on the ride to the mall that they didn't notice the radio wasn't playing. They had been chatting none stop since arriving at the airport that morning. However, the whole time Bobbi was contemplating when she would share her news about Savon.

Nikki parked at the food court entrance at the mall. They both checked their make-up in the rearview mirror and went inside. Before they could make it through the door good, a worker from the Chinese food counter practically shoved a sample of Bourbon chicken down their throats. It was so good they decided to grab lunch before shopping.

Bobbi got her tray first and headed for a table in the center of the food court away from the other patrons. Nikki could be a bit loud and dramatic when she wanted to so Bobbi hoped to keep the embarrassment to a minimum. As soon as they started eating Bobbi dropped the bomb.

"I slept with Savon."

Nikki nearly choked on a mouth full of rice. "Say what?!" She coughed to clear her throat. "Nooo... Please tell me you didn't." Nikki wiped her mouth. "When, Bobbi?"

"Last Saturday when I went to his house to tell him about the DNA results." Bobbi didn't feel guilty or bad about what she'd done. "It was an exciting time; you know. One thing led to the next, and his tongue was down my throat." Bobbi tingled at the thought.

"First of all, I don't understand how your client's tongue ended up in your mouth, but more importantly, you said you 'slept' with him. So when did that happen? And stop holding back on the info." Nikki wanted to be upset with Bobbi because her girl deserved more than another woman's seconds, but she couldn't. This wasn't the Bobbi she knew—the go-getter with a heart of steel. Emotions never played a part in Bobbi's romantic relationships, but here she was almost giddy.

For the next hour, Bobbi told Nikki about her encounters with Savon—how she whipped a u-turn to go back to his house the first time and everything. She even shared how much she enjoyed spending time with him and how he was the perfect gentleman, always considerate and respectful.

When Nikki asked about his fiancée, Bobbi said she wasn't sure what their status was. The times he vented about his relationship with Monica, Bobbi only listened. Besides, nothing about Monica was of any interest to her, especially since she disrespected her when they first met.

Nikki really didn't know what to say. It wasn't that she judged Bobbi; but rather the whole situation sounded like a recipe for disaster. And she didn't want her friend to be caught in the middle. Monica definitely sounded like a hot-head from what Bobbi had said about her; and although Bobbi was level headed and even tempered, she could be off the chain if provoked.

They finished lunch and strolled through the mall, the conversation still on Savon. Nikki didn't think Savon was fair by not being clear to Bobbi about his intentions—whatever they were. Taking Bobbi out for dinner and literally treating her like she was his fiancée rather than Monica was selfish. Now her best friend was getting emotions for him whether she realized it or not, and that concerned Nikki.

In the *Nordstrom* shoe department Bobbi and Nikki checked out the summer clearance racks them tried on boots to add to their collection. Two pairs of shoes later for Nikki and a pair of boots for Bobbi, the two moved on to the make-up counter. They tried on the new Fall lipstick and lip gloss shades. Bobbi purchased more of the pink sheer gloss she loved, while Nikki decided on a coral lipstick and liner.

Leaving the make-up counter, Bobbi didn't look up as she put her credit card back inside her wallet. When she took her third step she collided with another shopper who wasn't paying attention.

"Excuse me," Bobbi said. When she looked up, the pair of eyes looking back at her belonged to Monica.

Chapter 32

Monica's lips were formed to say excuse me until she realized it was Bobbi—the woman her man introduced her to while they were out to dinner a few months ago. The look on Monica's face reminded Bobbi of how disrespectful she had been the first time they met. But Bobbi was willing to give Monica the benefit of the doubt and chop it up as a bad day.

She casually pointed towards Monica. "I know you, you're Monica, right? Savon's fiancée? We met in DC over the summer."

Monica glanced at her two friends then back at Bobbi. "Yes, I remember you," she said in a dry uninspired tone.

Bobbi looked at Nikki who was trying to hold back her distaste for Monica's attitude. Bobbi felt the same way. It took considerable self control for her not to enlighten Monica about her wack ass attitude, and how she had been taking real good care of Savon since she ran off and left him alone in his troubles. But she figured eventually, if she kept seeing Savon, the opportunity to share her thoughts with Monica would come again. So she would wait.

Monica smiled a fake smile at Bobbi and Nikki and asked her two girlfriends if they were ready to go. Both her friends were attractive, tall model types like her. They also glanced at Bobbi and Nikki before the three of them burst out laughing and walked off.

Nikki grabbed Bobbi by the arm and they walked in the opposite direction back into the mall.

"I have one question. Have you gotten Savon out of your system, because Monica is going to be trouble?"

"What do you mean?" asked Bobbi.

"Are you serious? That bitch is crazy. And if you keep dealing with Savon she's bound to find out. Then what?"

Bobbi didn't seem phased one bit. "Does it look like I care?" She looked at Nikki with a blank expression. "I mean really. Monica's game is all busted up. She ran off like a spoiled brat and left her man to deal with his troubles alone. It just so happened that during the course of working through everything, he found comfort in the way I listened and treated him. I didn't deliberately go after him. So when and if she finds out what happened and tries to step to me, I'll cross that bridge then. But please understand. I don't plan to play hide and seek for her or Savon."

"Well. I guess you told me," Nikki joked. She knew Bobbi better than anyone, which meant she knew her friend didn't sleep around with married men or men who were obviously attached. So Savon must have really touched something deep within her for anything to jump off between them.

"Sooo... You ready to go get our cook on? I'm sure everybody is waiting to see us." Nikki asked.

"Let's ride," Bobbi said. She pushed all thoughts of Monica out of her head and put her mind on things that mattered, like visiting with her family.

Chapter 33

Weeks had passed since Bobbi last saw Tony. They had managed to catch up with each other a couple of times over the telephone long enough to say what's up, but work had them both too busy to actually get together. That's why when Tony called to ask if she wanted to have dinner and check out a movie she was thrilled.

Finally she would be in the presence of a man who could provide a distraction from her thoughts of Savon, who by the way she hadn't heard from since the night of their celebration dinner, three weeks ago.

Bobbi dressed in a pair of boot cut jeans, a rust-colored cashmere sweater and four inch brown angle boots. Instead of wearing her hair strait she wore loose body curls that hung to the middle of he back, no bangs. She grabbed her Gucci hobo curse and headed out the door.

When she talked to Tony earlier that morning, she told him that she would meet him at his house. He lived closer to the movie theater and the restaurant they planned to go to away. When she arrived he let her inside and they embraced the way friends do when they haven't seen each other for a while. Tony brushed a quick kiss to her lips.

She followed him into the kitchen as they talked about what movie they were going to see. Bobbi took a seat on a stool at the breakfast bar in front of Tony's open laptop. He asked her to check the show times for the movie she wanted to see while he went upstairs to get his wallet.

When he returned they left the house in his black 750 BMW, and headed for the movie theater.

Later for dinner, they went to a quaint bistro with a live jazz band. It was one of their favorite spots when they wanted to listen to music. After they ordered their meals, they talked about work and their mutual acquaintances. As much as she hoped it wouldn't come up, Tony asked about Savon and his past troubles. She realized everyone knew she represented him because she was with him on television during the press conference. However, she was trying to get Savon out of her head and it was actually working until now.

Bobbi pointed at a man dancing old school in the small area next to the band. Savon turned to look and they both laughed. The band was extraordinary and Bobbi had been tapping her foot and grooving in her seat since they sat down. When she heard them play the first bar of a familiar ballad, she asked Tony to dance with her.

On the dance floor, he pulled her to him and they held each other closely as they swayed to the sultry sound of the saxophone. He rubbed her back slowly and kissed her ear. From that moment on, her attention was tuned to him and him alone. They danced for two more songs—one slow and one fast. When they returned to their table, the server had just arrived with their dinner plates.

On the short ride back to his house, Tony played jazz in the CD player. Bobbi leaned back in her seat and listened to the smooth tunes. The night had been wonderful. She was really thankful for a male friend like Tony. They never had any drama. Everything was fun and easy with him: sex, talking, companionship. She smiled.

At his house, he opened her car door and reached for her hand, continuing to hold it as they entered the house from the garage. It could be perceived as an odd gesture considering they weren't emotionally connected—but not for them. Their fingers intertwined let her know that he wasn't ready for her to leave—that he wanted more.

First they stopped in the kitchen for water then he led her upstairs to his bedroom. He put their water bottles on the nightstand and pulled her to him.

"I waited all night for this," he whispered against her lips.

Bobbi wrapped her arms around his neck as he leaned down to kiss her. He undressed her, pulled the covers back and laid her down on his king sized bed before undressing himself. For the next hour he showed her just how much he missed being with her in their special way.

The rise and fall of Tony's chest as he slept created a peaceful backdrop for Bobbi's thoughts. Why was she thinking about Savon? He obviously wasn't thinking about her or he would have called. She let out a deep sigh. The clock on Tony's dresser read midnight. Should she get dressed and go home or stay?

She decided to leave so she rolled out of Tony's arms, but not before kissing him on the cheek, and went to the bathroom. She cleaned herself up, put on her clothes and went back into the bedroom. She patted Tony's shoulder to wake him so he could walk her out.

Still drowsy, he glanced at the clock. "Baby you don't have to leave. It's too late for you to be driving home anyway." He yawned. "Get back in bed." He turned over and went back to sleep.

Bobbi sat on the bed. "Tony, get up. I know it's late but I want to go home." She smacked his butt. "Come on man, get up."

"Okay, okay," he said barely able to hold his eyes open. He threw on some sweats and his slippers and walked her out to her car parked at the curb. He opened her car door then kissed her on the forehead. "Call me when you get home."

"Alright, sleepy head." She kissed him back, got in the car and headed home.

Chapter 34

Bobbi listened to hip hop on her way home to help her stay awake. She was grooving and rapping when she heard her Blackberry ring. Who could be calling her at this hour? It was twelve thirty. She reached inside her purse thinking it was probably Tony calling to talk to her until she made it home.

When she read the display her heart skipped a beat. It was Savon. She muted her music wondering if she should answer. It had been damn near a month since she heard from him, and now he was calling her after midnight? She decided to see what he could possible be calling for this late.

"Hello," she answered unenthused—not excited not irritated, just neutral.

"What's up Bobbi? How are you? It's Savon," he said trying to sound upbeat.

Was that the best he could do? "Hi stranger. I'm well. And to what do I owe this midnight call? You do realize it's almost one A.M.?" She wasn't letting him off that easy.

He cleared his throat. "I need to talk to you. Can I come over?"

"Come over? What's going on?" She switched into publicist mode right away. "Has something else come up with the paternity situation?"

"No, no. It's nothing like that." He took a deep breath. "Monica is tripping. She told me she saw you in Atlanta last weekend and asked if I was sleeping with you. What happened? Did you say something to her?"

Bobbi became irritated with his question. "Wait a minute Savon. I don't know where you're going with this, but let me make something crystal clear for you. Whatever is going on between you and Monica is just that; don't pull me into it. I ran into her at the mall and all I did was speak. She acted like a pure dee fool and that was the extent of my conversation with her. So if she feels insecure about y'alls relationship that's your fault, not mine. So I can't help you with that."

"Okay Bobbi." Savon hadn't expected that response. He figured he would question Bobbi and find out that she led Monica to believe the two of them had something going on. What he hadn't calculated was her shutting his whole conversation down. "I still would like to talk to you though. Can I come over?"

"Look Savon. I'm not home right now but when I get there I'm going strait to bed. Why don't we meet for lunch tomorrow?" Bobbi didn't have the patience to continue this insane conversation. "Call me in the morning and let me know where you want to meet, okay?"

Unwillingly, Savon conceded. "Alright. I'll call you tomorrow."

"Good night," Bobbi said ending the call as she pulled into her garage.

Bobbi called Tony to let him know she was home. He was barely conscious when she called. She laughed as she hung up the phone. *He probably won't even remember that I called*, she thought.

She said her prayers and got in bed. With her hands behind her head she stared up at the ceiling. What else could Savon possibly have to say? She exhaled. After tomorrow, Bobbi didn't care if they ever got together again. He was already becoming too much drama. At lunch she would give him the opportunity to get whatever he was compelled to say off of his chest and that would be it.

His problems with Monica were not hers, and she refused to get caught up in their drama. If he wanted to spend time with her, Monica would have to be demoted. In other words, he would have to drop her ass back to second string. Bottom line.

Chapter 35

After church, Bobbi met Savon for lunch at the *Cheesecake Factory*. He was already there waiting when she arrived. He greeted her when she walked in the door.

"Hey Bobbi. You look nice," He complimented, admiring her church look. He brushed a kiss to her right cheek and inhaled her scent. This woman was delicious, he thought.

Bobbi smiled. "Hey yourself."

The hostess led them to a booth in the bar area and handed them menus. Savon never took his eyes off of Bobbi.

"So did you ask me to come here so you could stare at me or are we here to talk?" she asked with a smirk on her face.

Savon chuckled. "For the record I'm not staring at you. I was noticing how you changed your hair. I can see more of your face now." He nodded in approval. "It's nice."

Their server walked up and asked for their drink order. They both asked for water with lemon and placed their food orders as well. As soon as the server left the table Bobbi responded to Savon's last comment.

"Thank you." Bobbi wasn't flattered to be honest. She was on guard more than anything, especially after hearing about Monica and her shenanigans last night. "I'm quite sure we're not here for you to shower me with compliments so what's up for real?"

Savon exhaled. He told Bobbi about how Monica wasn't returning any of his calls so he'd stopped calling her as much. Matter of fact, he only called her once the first week he was on travel and that's when she told him that she needed her space to think things through. Next thing he knew she was calling asking if he was sleeping with Bobbi.

Monica told Savon that she had a feeling something might be going on between the two of them the first time she met Bobbi. But after running into her in Atlanta at the mall she was convinced of it. When Savon told her there was nothing going on, she threw a fit, yelling and screaming into the telephone. He tried to calm her down but she wouldn't listen to reason so he hung up on her. They didn't talk again until Savon was back home from his two-week travel and she told him that she was coming to DC so they could talk in person. Savon finished his story up by telling Bobbi that Monica would be back in DC within the next couple of days.

The server returned with lunch which gave Savon an opportunity to regroup after all he'd said.

"That sure was a mouth full," Bobbi said. She was a little heated with his put-her-on-notice talk, but she didn't let it show. The nerve of this joker to think he could control her by telling her that his woman would be back on the scene.

Bobbi looked at her salad and decided she wasn't hungry any more. When she looked up at Savon who wasn't eating either, she knew she had to enlighten him on just who she was and where she stood on the situation.

"Savon, so that you are completely clear," Bobbi started in a no nonsense I mean business tone, "I don't sneak around or duck and dodge anyone—man or woman. I call the shots in my life and no one else. You and I had our fling or whatever you want to call it because I decided that's what I wanted—not because you made the first move. I went against everything I stand for as a woman when I decided to sleep with you knowing you were engaged, but that's on me. But please understand that you and Monica and what you decide to do with each other is not of concern to me. You have far too much drama with you for us to have anything going on."

Bobbi took the napkin from her lap and placed it on the table, then pushed her chair back.

"I have to go now, but I wish you and your situation all the best. And for the record, this conversation doesn't change anything for me professionally. As your publicist I will go above and beyond to keep your reputation flawless." She smiled and extended her right hand.

"Friends?"

"Friends." Savon shook Bobbi's hand as she stood up. He didn't know what in the hell just happened. He brought her here to make sure she wasn't expecting anything from him even though they had been intimate and spent a lot of time together, especially with Monica coming back. But somehow she had flipped the script, again. He was lost for words.

"Take care, Savon," were Bobbi's last words before she left him standing there at the table, jaw hanging on the floor.

Chapter 36

The following weekend, Bobbi, Gavin, Nikki and her friend Todd met at Indi Blu to celebrate Bobbi's Birthday. She really wasn't in the mood to make a fuss over her big day, but Nikki insisted on getting together with a few friends for dinner and drinks.

The four sat in a huge circular booth close to the bar. During dinner they all talked about current events, sports and the latest gossip around town, especially in their social circle. But after dinner, things paired off and Nikki and her boo, Todd, were deep in conversation while Bobbi laughed and talked with Gavin.

Todd was older than them, maybe mid thirties, with a settled kind of vibe about him. Just like Nikki liked her men. Younger guys were too silly for her, especially since she had enough jokes for everybody. Todd was tall and handsome, well groomed with curly hair and a mustache. His style was like something off the pages of *GQ Magazine,* which complimented Nikki perfectly.

Spending time with true friends was a breath of fresh air for Bobbi. So much of her time was devoted to people-pleasing and stroking egos that it was like finding and old friend when she could just be herself. She was grateful Nikki had talked her into coming out tonight.

The freckled face server came up to their table. "Is everything okay?"

"Another bottle of Champaign, please," requested Gavin after receiving nods of approval from everyone at the table.

"Coming right up," the server responded.

Nikki and Bobbi were talking when the server returned with the bottle. Nikki was happy to see Bobbi enjoying herself. Even though she tried to mask her feelings, Nikki knew she was a bit down about Savon and how he treated their intimacy like it meant nothing to him. Bobbi was definitely a tough cookie; but even the toughest cookie could be broken.

Gavin interrupted them to make a toast. He filled their glasses and they all lifted them towards the center of the table.

"Here's to you Bobbi," he started, looking into her eyes, "wishing you the best on your special day and wishes for many more." Gavin threw his arm around her shoulder pulling her into him. He kissed her on the cheek as all four glasses clinked.

"Thanks sweetie." She smiled back at him and kissed him back on the cheek.

"Hey, hey. Cut that incest crap out. I keep telling y'all that family shouldn't be kissing on each other like that," Nikki, joked.

Gavin smiled at Bobbi and winked. When she smiled back at him he leaned his face toward hers and she pecked his lips making a loud kissing sound. Since his arm was already around her shoulders he squeezed her to him. They both smiled at Nikki.

Nikki looked from Gavin to Bobbi. "Alright keep it up. Keep acting like the two of you have something going on and I'll tell everybody in the family. And you know you won't get any peace after that. Everyone will want to know when the wedding is."

"Girl, chill," Gavin said to his cousin; his arm still around Bobbi. You know we're just playing around.

"Yeah, lighten up girl." Bobbi tapped Nikki on the arm.

"Mmm-hmm. I hear you," Nikki replied in a condescending tone. She sipped her champagne, looking over the rim of her glass. "I have my eyes on you two."

Gavin, Bobbi and Todd laughed.

Across the restaurant in a dimly lit corner, Savon sat at a table with Monica. From the time the hostess had seated them an hour ago, his eyes were on Bobbi and her friends. Bobbi was his fantasy in living color. Sure, Monica was attractive with her tall, thin frame and long auburn hair, but her attitude was a turn off.

For a man in Savon's position, women came a dime a dozen if he wanted them to. So he had come to a place in his life where he wanted a woman with something more to offer than just a hot body and a pretty face. He needed to be able to talk to her and truly enjoy her company. And that's what pulled on him about Bobbi. Her attitude and temperament were the exact opposite of Monica's. She was cool as hell to hang out with and she kept her cool no matter what.

Savon figured the dude sitting between Bobbi and Nikki was there with Nikki, but he wondered why Gavin was hanging all over Bobbi. And why had she just kissed him on the lips?

Although he and Gavin weren't the best of friends, as teammates they respected each other. They had even hung out after a few games with other teammates. That's how he knew that Gavin and Nikki were actually blood cousins and that he considered Bobbi to be his family too.

Savon wanted to go over and speak, to see how Bobbi would respond to him, but he couldn't chance Monica's reaction. So far he was pretty sure she hadn't noticed that Bobbi was even there. And if he could help it, she never would. He didn't want to argue about Bobbi tonight or listen to Monica babbling on about how she didn't like Bobbi.

Monica had just come back to DC three days ago and it had taken him until tonight to calm her down enough for them to have a peaceful dinner out on the town. Tonight not even Bobbi with her fine ass was worth disturbing this moment after all the grief Monica had given him.

Somehow he'd have to find a way to talk to her soon because he missed their connection terribly.

Chapter 37

The brisk November air in DC was a chilling reminder that winter was on its way. Savon and Monica parked and moved swiftly towards the entrance to the restaurant.

Savon had just returned from an away game so he and Monica where out celebrating his return and a crucial win for the Warriors.

Football season was almost over and the Warriors were fighting for their spot in the play-offs. Savon was desperately trying to hold it together on the field and at home but Monica wasn't making it easy.

A month had passed since she moved back in with him and he was pretty sure that he wanted to call the engagement off. Although they were in the same house, sleeping in the same bed, nothing was happening between them. Thankfully she had dismissed the paternity situation, but now her focus was centered on whether or not he slept with Bobbi. She questioned him relentlessly. As if that wasn't enough, she was still withholding the goodies.

Savon missed Bobbi more than ever. Other than a few business conversations over the telephone which he initiated, he hadn't spent any time with her or even had the pleasure of hearing her laugh. True enough, she was cordial when they spoke, but there was nothing special about the way she talked to him.

He didn't feel that spark of excitement in her voice when she realized it was him on the other end. For reasons he couldn't explain, that bothered him.

Monica was talking to him about an entrée on the menu, but his thoughts were elsewhere. There was no doubt that he loved Monica, but things between them had become so complicated that he was beginning to think the relationship wasn't worth salvaging. They were different as night and day and by all indications, growing apart. He exhaled. What was he going to do about her? And more importantly, how was he going to get back in Bobbi's good graces.

Savon and Monica placed their orders and made small talk. He sipped on Hennessey, and she had a glass of wine while they waited for their meals to arrive.

"Have you decided if you're going home for Thanksgiving yet?" Monica asked.

"Not yet. But I'm pretty sure I'm not going. I need to stay focused right now and I can do that best if I stay here."

Monica rolled her eyes upward slightly irritated. "So when are we going to go home together, Savon? After everything that's happened, you never once came to Atlanta to see about me—just to see if I was okay. I think we need to go home together soon, and next week for Thanksgiving would be perfect. Everybody would be able to see that we are still together despite the baby momma drama you put me through."

"Monica, you know I can't just up and go wherever I want during the season. This is my job. This is what I do for a living. I have a contract to honor." He tried not to get frustrated with her. "I called you more times than I can count and you wouldn't even answer the phone." All he wanted to do was have a nice dinner and enjoy her company. But she was making that an impossible possibility.

"If you loved me, you would have come." She paused for effect. "And if you want this relationship to have a chance you need to reconsider about going home with me next week. I feel like I'm in this relationship by myself most of the time any way. You haven't been home with me since June and that was only for a day." She looked him square in the eyes. "I'm getting tired of this, Savon."

If he thought she was going to play second to his career, he was mistaken. In case he hadn't recognized, any man would be thrilled to have her as his future wife. She was beautiful, successful and she came from good stock; which meant she could also give him beautiful babies if she decided to. So he'd better get it together real soon or she was going to call the whole thing off, for good.

Savon had smoke coming from his ears by the time Monica finished her "come to Jesus" speech. The only reason he hadn't called off the engagement so far was that he still felt confused about what he wanted. Even with all of her flaws and drama, until now he had convinced himself that Monica wouldn't try to drain his bank account if things didn't work out. But now he wasn't so sure. The more problems they had the more he discovered about Monica that concerned him.

"Salmon?" the thin lanky server asked looking at Savon. And here's your pecan encrusted chicken salad ma'am," he said to Monica. "Will there be anything else?"

Savon took a bite of his salmon. "Can I get some more sauce for my salmon?"

"Sure. I'll be right back."

Savon had a mouth full when the waiter returned with his sauce. He looked up and nodded thank you. Just as the server walked away, Savon's eyes caught a glance of the entrance to the restaurant. He couldn't believe his eyes. He almost choked on his dinner.

Chapter 38

Tony grabbed Bobbi's hand as they entered the restaurant. The two had been out all day celebrating his promotion to junior partner. Now Bobbi was treating him to dinner at the same restaurant Savon had taken her to in celebration of his name being cleared of paternity.

As soon as Tony called and told her his good news, she made reservations. All he knew is that they were going to dinner after finishing all the festivities he had planned for the day. She told him dinner was on her.

The lights were dim like she remembered, evoking romance and closeness. Tony held her hand until they reached their table. The hostess gave them menus and left.

Tony looked around the restaurant. "I'm impressed. How did you get reservations here on such short noticc? My firm has brought a few high powered clients here for lunch, so I know how hard it is to get in without at least a two week notice. That is unless you're on the who's who list of important people."

"Don't worry about that Attorney Weldon. I got this." She smiled and winked at him. "Just enjoy the moment."

On the other side of the restaurant Savon couldn't keep his eyes off of Bobbi. His appetite seemed to dissipate after he saw her hand-in-hand with the *Morris Chestnut* look alike. He couldn't believe how comfortable they seemed with each other.

Why hadn't she told him she was seeing someone? In all the time they spent together he never got the sense that Bobbi was seriously involved with someone. And that's exactly how things appeared to him right now.

Monica frowned at Savon. "Is something wrong with your food? You stopped eating."

"Nah...it's good. Didn't you see how fast I was eating? I need to slow it down before I choke to death." He chuckled. The last thing he wanted to do was bring attention to Bobbi. Good thing Monica's back was to the other side of the restaurant. As long as he played it cool she would never notice what was up.

Tony ordered a bottle of wine for him and Bobbi. She made a toast to his promotion and they both took a sip. After they ordered dinner, Tony excused himself to use the restroom. Bobbi sat at the table enjoying the melodic chords of the piano as she glanced around the restaurant. She nodded at a business associate she noticed a few tables over.

When Savon returned to the table he reached for Bobbi's hand. He told her how much it meant to him for her to spend the day with him and how he appreciated her making arrangements for dinner.

Bobbi was touched by his sentiment. This was definitely one of the reasons why she liked him and they were able to keep things going with minimal drama. He always showed appreciation for anything she did for him. It was never a thought that he would take advantage of her kindness or expect more than she was willing to give.

When their food arrived, Bobbi moved her chair closer to his so she could feed him. A gesture the two laughed about. It was just one more way for her to treat him special on his special night.

Savon was about to loose it when he saw Tony holding Bobbi's hand at the table. Who was this cat, he wondered. When he looked over at them again she was feeding him. Savon was about to come unglued. And he could hardly focus on Monica because of it. He hoped she wasn't picking up on his behavior, but it was getting harder by the minute to keep his emotions under wraps.

Bobbi and Tony continued to enjoy their evening together throughout dinner while Savon was tortured by their presence. Unbeknownst to him, his preoccupation with someone or something else on the other side of the restaurant wasn't lost on Monica. She was nobody's fool. Now in his selfish desire to have his cake and eat it too, he was caught slipping.

"Savon!" Monica called out trying to get his attention. When he didn't answer she followed his stare across the room to look directly into Bobbi's eyes.

Monica was fuming. She looked at Savon. "So that's why you can't stay focused on what's going on at your own table." She saw red. "Take me home right now," she exclaimed.

Savon didn't know what to do. He never meant for Monica to figure out that he had been fixated on Bobbi most of the night. Hurting her was never his intention, but somehow it kept happening. He also didn't want Bobbi to know that he was there with Monica, but just before Monica realized what was going on, so did Bobbi. Their eyes locked and neither broke the stare.

Monica was half way to the door when Savon caught up to her. He reached for her arm to try and slow her down but she snatched away giving him a look that dared him to touch her again. When they got to the truck and Savon hit the remote to unlock the doors, she nearly broke the latch snatching the door open.

Savon didn't dare get in her way right now. He was pretty sure he saw steam coming from her nose and ears when she left the table. It was definitely his fault that she was so upset and he sincerely regretted it. Now, if only he could get her home without having to be closed in the same car with her was his greatest wish.

The radio filled the awkward space between them until Monica turned it off saying she needed to get something off of her chest. She turned to face Savon.

"I get it now. You don't want to get married—you never did. You just want to hang on to me so nobody else can have me while you strut around DC passing out dick to everyone you meet."

She wanted to claw his eyeballs out, but didn't have the fight in her—at least not anymore. So she turned the radio back on and sat there; her emotions bubbling over the brim.

Savon had taken her through too much over the last two years. There was always some woman giving him the eye when they were out. And here lately it was the paternity issue, and now this bold bitch, Bobbi. Enough was enough.

When they made it home Monica jumped out of the car and went inside before Savon had a chance to turn it off. He was glad she did because he couldn't take any more confrontation right now. He turned off the car, put in a jazz CD, leaned back in his seat and closed his eyes.

How was he going to get out of this one? One thing Monica said was true: he did want her, but he also wanted Bobbi now.

Bobbi had showed him that he wasn't ready to marry Monica with all their differences. Yet at the same time, he didn't want anyone else to be with her. Savon blew out a deep breath and opened his eyes. *Guess I better get in here and take my bashing like a man*, he thought.

By the time he made it inside, Monica was coming down the stairs with one suitcase in-hand and another one already sitting at the bottom of the staircase.

"Where are you going," he asked, not wanting to deal with this scene again.

"Back to Atlanta." She never skipped a beat. She didn't look up at him or acknowledge him standing there when she pulled her bags to sit at the front door.

He grabbed her arm. "Wait. Can we talk about this?"

"Humph. Talk? So now you want to talk? Fuck you, Savon!" She slapped his face hard then stepped closer until they were nose width apart. Her chest was heaving. "I sat in that damn restaurant with you for over an hour and you barely said a word to me. But I guess you couldn't since you were caught up watching your girlfriend while she was out on a date with the next man. Dumb ass..." She walked off.

Savon was getting mad now. He couldn't believe she slapped him. If she hadn't been so jealous and self centered in their relationship, another woman could never have gotten close to him. If she wanted to leave, the door was open, but she could rest assured that he wouldn't be calling her to come back this time.

"You know what Monica? I'm sick of your jealousy and all of your drama. If you walk out on me this time, don't think about coming back." With that, he walked off and headed upstairs.

"I hate you!" Monica screamed through tears. She fumbled to pull off her engagement ring and then threw it at him. The three carat emerald cut diamond hit the back of his neck and cut him, but he never turned around.

Monica broke down at the front door crying like a baby. She couldn't believe he had walked off from her like she was the one who was in the wrong. Although she didn't have proof he was sleeping with Bobbi, intuition told her all she needed to know. If he could be this cold towards her and she hadn't done anything to him but try to love him through all of his bull, then to hell with him.

When she heard a car horn blow, she peeked out the window to make sure it was her ride. She pulled herself together and opened the door to let the taxi driver know that she would be right out. Then she went to the bathroom to clean her face.

When she came out, she looked up at the stairs to see if Savon was there but he wasn't. Fresh tears fell as she grabbed here bags and went to catch her ride to the airport.

Chapter 39

Had Savon and Monica been sitting there in the restaurant the entire time? When Bobbi happened upon Savon's stare their eyes locked. She felt like she could hear his soul speaking to her. It was something about that man that pulled at her heart, and she didn't like it.

Bobbi rolled onto her back. She had been home from the restaurant for over an hour now and was lying across her bed thinking about what happened. Thank God Tony was oblivious to what was going on because she would have been disappointed if Savon and Monica had ruined his night.

Tony had dropped her off, kissed her goodnight and kept it moving. She wasn't in the mood for rocking and knocking boots tonight. Not after seeing Savon and the way he looked at her before chasing after Monica. Aside from the nonsense he'd been calling her about at work lately, they really hadn't talked. She hated to admit it, but seeing him tonight ignited something inside her.

Bobbi exhaled. *Why me*? She reached over and turned off the lamp on her nightstand. Savon really needed to tighten his game up if he was going to cheat on his fiancée. It just wasn't cool to have that kind of drama.

A ringing phone startled Bobbi out of her sleep. She looked at the clock—it was one thirty. *Who could be calling at this hour?* She rubbed her eyes, turned on the lamp and looked at the display screen. It was Savon.

"Yes?"

Savon was taken aback by Bobbi's greeting. He realized it was late and his call was unexpected, but damn. She said "yes." He started to rethink making the call.

"Savon. I know you didn't call me at oh-dark-thirty to breath into the phone." Bobbi's voice was slightly above a whisper, her hand rested on her forehead and her eyes were closed.

"Yeah, ahhh…what's up?

"For real? You mean you called me in the middle of the night to ask me what's up? I'm sleep, Savon. Correction—I was sleep." She wasn't going to cut him any slack. If he had something to say to her he would have to speak into the mic. In other words, man-up and spit it out. She didn't fare well with people who beat around the bush. It wasn't her style and she didn't believe it to be his either.

"I apologize for waking you, Bobbi. But whatever happened to answering the telephone with a simple 'hello'?" He regrouped and was back on his game again.

Bobbi yawned and sat up in bed. "You act like it's one in the afternoon. I already knew it was you. And based on the hour, you must have something to say you feel is so important it can't wait until a more reasonable hour. So 'yes' is more fitting than hello." Bobbi was wide awake now.

Savon chuckled. "Okay, Bobbi. I guess you have a point." He liked this woman. She knew how to make her point without all the drama and theatrics some women used.

"I have some things I want to say to you if you're willing to listen."

Her right eyebrow arched. She didn't know what to expect. "Okay." She drew her knees up to her chest and got comfortable.

For a good while, Savon told Bobbi about his relationship with Monica, how they met and why he asked her to marry him. After running across his share of gold diggers, meeting Monica, who was not only gorgeous but accomplished, and had her own money; was like finding a diamond in a lump of coal.

Savon told her that they had been engaged for a year but had yet to set a date for the wedding, which was primarily due to him moving to DC. The plan was for him to get settled in first then they would decide if the wedding would be in Atlanta or DC. But the paternity trouble started right after he bought the house and changed everything.

He told Bobbi that Monica had started acting jealous as soon as he gave her the ring. However, he admitted that being in that serious of a commitment was new to him and he had messed up a few times but for the most part he had been faithful.

Bobbi remained silent as he continued. He said that when he saw her at the restaurant tonight he realized that he wasn't ready for marriage at all—at least not right now. And that he wasn't sure Monica was the one for him anymore. He told Bobbi that he wanted the opportunity to get to know her without limitation.

Lastly, he told Bobbi about his confrontation with Monica after they left the restaurant. He said that he gave her an ultimatum to stay and work things out or the engagement was off. Then he told her that Monica had thrown her engagement ring at him and left.

Once he was finished with his story he asked Bobbi his burning question.

"So was dude at the restaurant someone you're serious about?"

"He's a very dear friend." Bobbi paused to gather her thoughts. "I know you asked a simple question, but I need to explain some things about myself in order for you to understand who Tony is to me."

This was unfamiliar territory for Bobbi. Why did Savon feel the need to be so intimate and transparent with her? Although she avoided emotional exchange with men it didn't mean she didn't have feelings. Actually, it was quite the opposite; her heart was very sensitive. When she loved, she loved hard. And that had proven to be a very hurtful and painful quality in her past. Therefore, she guarded her heart with a brick wall. Now here was Savon chiseling away at it bit by bit.

She took a deep breath and proceeded to tell Savon about Tony and how they weren't in a committed relationship. That their arrangement was more about obliging each other's needs in the bedroom but they genuinely liked each other. She told him that they had been friends for almost three years and tonight they were out celebrating a promotion for him at work. She told Savon that she was single and free to date and to do whatever she wanted.

Savon tried to process what she said but he wasn't sure he believed her—at least not the part about her and Tony only being friends. He especially didn't like the part about them taking care of each other in the bedroom. But he would find out soon enough because he had plans to turn up the heat and see just what kind of woman Bobbi really was, and if there was more to what he felt for her.

Chapter 40

After that late night telephone call from Savon, Bobbi began to wonder if it was possible to trust him with her heart. For three hours he talked about his life, mistakes with women including Monica, and his thoughts and feelings about her. Honestly, it blew her mind.

Bobbi was used to men complimenting her about her looks, her business acumen, and even her skills between the sheets. But it chipped away at huge chucks of her heart to hear Savon say how he felt about her. He told her that he would never forget the way she supported him through the paternity accusations where everyone else had questioned his innocence and integrity, including his fiancée and closest friends. He said that she had allowed him to bend her ear, unloading his concerns and troubles nearly everyday during the ordeal and never showed that she was tired of listening, even if she was.

Now that Savon had spilled his guts, they were spending all of their free time together. Since both of them had demanding schedules, it usually amounted to dinner a few nights a week and whatever time thcy could squeeze on weekends. Yet it was enough time for Savon to know that he wanted more.

True to his promise, Savon had not called Monica since she left his house in a taxi four weeks ago. And just as well, he hadn't heard from her either. Christmas was only a week away and he wanted to step things up with Bobbi. He needed to know if they could handle the realities of each other's lives without any outside distractions. He wanted to be exclusive.

But telling her of his intentions would have to wait until after the holidays. They were both spending Christmas in Atlanta with their families, plus his final game of the season was at the end of the month. New Year's Eve would be the perfect time to let her know what was on his mind and start the New Year off right.

Chapter 41

Is this real, Bobbi thought. Could Savon really be the caring, sensitive man he keeps showing her? In her gut she believed he was. Now here she was lying across his chest while he slept with a grin plastered on her face bright enough to light up New York City.

Last night Savon had told her that he wanted them to be exclusive. That he wanted them to see if they could work in a committed relationship. A million thoughts passed through her mind as he kissed every inch of her face, whispering his thoughts against her skin. Her head was spinning. At first she was afraid to answer him because to say yes would mean she had to let her guard down. But there was no way she could tell this man no. He treated her so special. But more importantly, she couldn't deny how she felt about him.

After she agreed to be with him, he showed her just how much she meant to him all night long. One orgasm after the next wracked her body while he talked to her above a whisper about his plans for their future. Just the thought of it made her quiver. She didn't think it was possible to feel this way about a man. Finally, love had found her.

Bobbi closed her eyes, still grinning. It was only six A.M. She'd wake Savon in a couple of hours so they could shower and go back to bed.

"United Flight 1507 to Washington, DC now boarding at Gate 12," announced the attendant.

Monica handed her boarding pass to the attendant at the gate and made her way down the ramp to her seat. She loaded her carry-on bag into the overhead compartment and buckled herself in for her surprise trip to see Savon.

When he came to Atlanta for Christmas he didn't bother to come see her or even pick up the phone to call. Everybody knew they weren't together anymore and that he had come home and basically ignored her existence. Her family was asking questions and even blamed her, saying she ran him off with her mouth. She knew her attitude needed some work and that she had a tendency to be jealous at times, but Savon never reassured her when it came to other woman. There was always someone up in his face or some woman he had business with.

But Monica never thought he would give up on her. They had been through some trying times in the past but the last six months had been the worst. Although she didn't want to deal with him if he cheated on her with that tramp Bobbi, the alternative wasn't an option. She couldn't imagine her life without Savon. So if she had to swallow her pride and reach out to him so they could talk, then she would do just that.

In two hours she would be at his house and hopefully in his arms before the night was over.

Bobbi swatted at Savon. "Stop," she said playfully.

He smacked her on the ass again. This time it really sounded off as the warm water from the shower rolled down her backside.

Even though they had just finished another round of thumb-sucking sex, he was hungry for more.

"Stop playing, Savon." She was feeling just as horny and if he didn't stop rubbing his manhood up against her ass and smacking it like that, they would be christening his walk-in shower any minute.

"I can't help it," he said kissing the back of her neck. He grabbed her around the waist and pulled her into him. Bobbi moaned and her head fell back onto his shoulder. As both of his hands touched and teased the most sensitive places on her body, he whispered in her ear. "I can't get enough of you."

Bobbi turned around and Savon lifted her up so she could wrap her legs around his waist. His strokes were long and firm. As he drove them both to the brink, Bobbi squeezed her muscles as tightly as she could causing his climax milliseconds before hers. Weak in the knees, Savon lost his footing and slipped on the wet tile.

Bobbi screamed when she realized they were falling. But from the way they were positioned, she was straddling him when they landed. So it was Savon's butt that hit the shower floor with a thud. He grunted. The water was still spraying from the shower head. Bobbi moved a lock of wet hair from her eyes.

"Are you okay?" she asked holding back a snicker.

"Do you know who I am?" Savon asked with his chest puffed up. "I take harder hits than that on the field." He kissed Bobbi on the lips.

"Bobbi got up and extended both her hands to help him up.

Now with their thirst for each other quenched for the time being, Savon washed Bobbi's back and she washed his. Though it took quite a bit of restraint on both their parts, they managed to finish their showers.

At Baltimore International Airport, Monica picked up a rental and headed for Savon's house. She was a little nervous showing up unannounced because she hadn't talked to Savon since that last fight over a month ago. But she wouldn't let that stop her from going after what she wanted. It was New Year's Day—a time for new beginnings. And she was determined to convince Savon that he needed her as much as she needed him.

It was forty degrees and raining. The low gray clouds held the promise of all day showers. Monica smiled. It was the perfect weather to be inside cuddled up with your boo. With any luck, that's exactly how she and Savon would be before the night was over.

Monica looked at the clock on the dashboard. It was ten o'clock and she was pulling into Savon's subdivision. When she got to his street, she didn't see his truck in the driveway but figured it was parked in the garage. Where else would he be this early on a cold, rainy Saturday morning?

She pulled into the circular driveway, turned off the car and took a deep breath. Maybe she should call Savon to see how he would respond to her before knocking on the door. *Yeah, that's what I'll do.*

First she dialed the house phone then his cell. Voicemail kicked in on both. *Humph, that's odd.* Monica gave it some thought and decided to try knocking on the door. If he didn't answer she would just use her key and let herself inside. She didn't come all this way for nothing. So if he wasn't home she would make herself useful and cook them a nice lunch or perhaps dinner depending on what time he returned.

She smoothed down a few loose strands of hair in the rearview mirror and exited the car. At the door she took a death calming breath to settle the fluttering in her stomach, and knocked. There was no answer. She tried to peek through the privacy glass windows on either side of the door but she couldn't see anything. She glanced up and down the street to see if by chance he was driving up. Monica pulled her jacket together. It was too cold to just stand there waiting, especially if Savon wasn't home so she reached in her purse for the key and opened the door.

Savon lay in bed channel surfing while Bobbi blow dried her hair in the bathroom. He couldn't believe how things were happening between them. To his pleasant surprise she had even more layers to her personality than he'd expected. She was funny, loyal, and the sex went to a whole other level last night after he told her he wanted a commitment. The corners of his lips turned up at the thought, and he moved his free hand to rest in his boxers.

Downstairs, Monica pushed the door open slowly and peeked inside. Softly, she called out to Savon. When he didn't answer she stepped inside and closed the door. She went to the kitchen, then the family room. Hands on her hips, she began to think he wasn't home after all. *Ah-ha...the garage.* Monica went to the garage to see if his truck was there. Seeing his Escalade made the fluttering in her belly come back. But at least now she knew he was home—probably in bed fast asleep, she thought. Before she closed the door to the garage, she couldn't help but wonder when he'd bought the white Benz.

Once Bobbi finished her hair, she replaced the large striped towel wrapped around her body with a hot pink camisole and matching bikini panties. When she walked into the bedroom, Savon wanted her again.

"You are so sexy."

"I already know that," Bobbi said smiling.

Savon shook his head. "And you are very cocky." He loved that about her.

"Nope…confident. Just move over so I can get in."

She climbed in bed and they cuddled, playing with each other under the covers. Every time he did something that made her laugh she kissed him between her giggles. Bobbi was on cloud nine.

Half way up the staircase, Monica was pretty sure she heard the television playing in Savon's bedroom. Reality set in. Suddenly she was nervous again. She didn't know how he would react to her being there but she hoped he wouldn't throw her out before hearing what she had to say. Now standing outside his bedroom door she took a deep breath and turned the knob.

Chapter 42

What the fuck! From his vantage point, Savon was certain he saw his bedroom door open slightly. He jumped up and grabbed his gun from the nightstand drawer. Following suit, Bobbi jumped up too—her eyes moving frantically between Savon and the gun, but she never said a word. He motioned for her to go to the bathroom. He stood planted on the hinged side of the door so he could see the intruder before they saw him.

Monica opened the door a wee bit at first. Then she pushed it open a little wider and eased her head inside. The gun was in her face before Savon realized it was her.

"Monica?! What in the hell are you doing in my house?" he shouted lowering the gun. He was in shock.

Monica's heart nearly leaped from her chest. It took a minute before she was able to speak.

"Savon, I tried calling you to let you know I was here but you didn't answer. I even knocked on the front door before using my key." She started to lose momentum from the dead stare Savon burned into her. Her words trailed off.

Savon's jaws clenched. "Why would you think you could just walk into my house like this? I told you it was over when you left. Nothing has changed, Monica."

None of the conversation escaped Bobbi's ears. Almost as soon as she made it to the bathroom and closed the door, she heard Savon say Monica's name. So she cracked the door just enough to hear what they were saying without being noticed. This was the very type of scene she purposely avoided. Now her feelings for Savon had left her slipping and she was dead smack in the middle of a love triangle. She rolled her eyes upward. Why her? Damn.

Savon shook his head and turned away from Monica to put his gun back in the nightstand. It was at that moment that he remembered Bobbi was in the bathroom. He rubbed his hand over his head and looked toward the ceiling. He could use miraculous intervention right about now. He sat on the bed.

"Listen, Monica. I moved on. It's over. I wish you hadn't come here like this."

As soon as Bobbi heard his words she took a deep breath and reached for the door knob. It was now or never. Although she hated being in this predicament, she wasn't going to hide out in her man's bathroom like a punk. If Monica had words for her, let the games begin. Bobbi opened the door and stepped into the bedroom.

Monica's eyes narrowed to slits. She skimmed over Bobbi's almost naked body standing on the other side of the room. When she looked back at Savon she saw red.

"How could you, Savon!" she screamed.

The scene turned bad. Monica charged toward Savon. He jumped up off the bed to steady himself. She started swinging on him and yelling obscenities. He tried to restrain her but she was like a mad woman. When he was finally able to grab hold of her flailing arms, he held her wrists.

"Let me go, Savon," she demanded through clenched teeth. Tears stained her face.

When he did, she started looking for things to throw. She picked up his cell phone and threw it at him. Quickly, he put up his arm and it missed his face by an inch. She was crying uncontrollably now. Next she rushed over to his dresser where two of his most cherished art pieces and a vase given to him by his mother were sitting. With one sweep of her hand, the two art pieces crashed to the floor.

"Monica! What the fuck is wrong with you?" Savon exclaimed. He closed the distance between them when she picked up the vase. He grabbed both of her arms and held them tight.

"That's it, Monica! If you break one more damn thing in my—"

Monica was able to twist her arms out of his hands. She picked the vase back up and hurled it at the wall. It shattered into small pieces.

"Oooh!" Savon shouted. He reached for his head with both hands. He was so mad steam was rising up out of his head.

Bobbi couldn't believe her eyes. Either she was being *Punked* or she had just stepped into the *Twilight Zone*. In a way, she felt sorry for Monica because she remembered being in those same shoes a time or two. And even though she cared for Savon, karma was whipping his ass right now. But this was their battle, not hers. So as long as Monica kept all that vigor focused on Savon everything would be cool.

The sound of the crashing vase snatched Monica out of her wild spell. Now she was back in Savon's face yelling at him about Bobbi again.

"I knew you were fucking that fat bitch. That's why I never liked her desperate ass."

Bobbi's fists clenched but she didn't say anything. Instead she zoned in on Monica completely. She no longer saw Savon or anything else in the room, just Monica. On everything she loved, if Monica brought her skinny ass across the room to take a swing at her, her modeling career would be over.

Before Bobbi could finish her thought, Monica was walking towards her. The look in her eyes said "now I'll deal with you." Bobbi didn't flinch. Monica was up in her face asking why she couldn't get her own man. Bobbi could smell her breath but she still didn't say a word, which pissed Monica off even more.

"Bitch, did you hear what I said?"

As soon as Savon heard the word "bitch" he crossed the room to get between them.

"Move, Savon," she screamed stepping around him.

Monica was back in Bobbi's face. "What's wrong, bitch? You don't have anything to say now?" She pointed her finger in Bobbi's face. "All the other times I've seen you, you always had something to say; interrupting me and my man at dinner; sweating him whenever you see us out. Now a bitch—"

CRACK! Before she knew it, Bobbi had tagged Monica upside her big head and dropped her. The universe stood still. Savon was stunned. He didn't see it coming and obviously neither did Monica. But Bobbi had taken all she could take. Although she considered herself to be a mature, self-controlled person, there were only so many bitches she was going to be; especially with Monica up in her face.

"Damn, Bobbi. Why did you do that?" Savon looked at Monica lying lifeless on the floor. He rubbed his hands over his head. "Is she dead?"

"I know you're not asking me anything about that raggedy bitch," Bobbi said appalled. She massaged her knuckles. "I could care less if she takes another breath right now." Bobbi rolled her eyes at Savon and went to the bathroom. She locked the door.

Looking in the mirror she began to cry. *How did I get myself into this?* She sat on the toilet and dropped her face into her hands.

Savon was pacing the floor when Bobbi came out of the bathroom. He stared at her for a moment then shook his head.

"I checked her pulse. Thank God she's still alive." He said. "Why did you have to hit her like that?"

"Are you serious? You saw how she was disrespecting me. I understand that you let her beat up on you because you're a man, but she can't get up in my face calling me out of my name and pointing her finger in my face…" Bobbi was livid. "She better be glad I didn't punch her in her damn throat and put her ass to sleep for real."

"But Bobbi, she's stretched out on my floor unconscious. What am I supposed to do about that?" He brushed past Bobbi and walked over by the bathroom. "Ahhh!" he yelled, and punched a hole in the wall. "Damn!" His knuckles were bleeding.

Bobbi spun around when she heard the impact.

"So let me get this straight," she said. "You asked me to be your woman; then she comes to town unexpected and unannounced, and beats you up; she gets up in my face calling me names, and I'm just supposed to take it?" Bobbi's chest was heaving by the time she finished talking.

Savon looked at her from the corner of his eye and began pacing the floor again with his hands on his waist.

"Savon. Are you listening to me?"

He raised his hand and waved her off. "I don't have time for that Bobbi. Not right now."

Unbelievable, she thought. Bobbi went into the bathroom, pulled a paper cup from the dispenser next to the sink and filled it with water. Then she went back into the bedroom with the cup of water in hand. She looked at Savon then poured the water on Monica's face.

"Are you crazy?!" he exclaimed. He hurried over to her and snatched the cup from her hand.

Bobbi didn't say a word. Instead she grabbed her clothes and got dressed. As she packed her overnight bag, Savon was down on the floor helping Monica regain consciousness. "I can't believe this shit," she said under her breath. By the time she had her things together, Monica was sitting up and Savon was catering to her. From what she could tell, it looked like Monica's nose was broken. *Humph. Serves her right.*

Savon lifted Monica off the floor and sat her up on the bed. When Monica realized Bobbi was still there she tried to say something but the pounding in her head wouldn't let her. All she managed to get out of her mouth was that nasty word bitch again. Before she could reach for her throbbing head, Bobbi was in her face.

"Look bitch," Bobbi said pointing her finger in Monica's face. "I tried to let you and Savon handle your drama between the two of you, but you wouldn't leave me out of it. Keep running that mouth and you'll be kissing the carpet again."

Savon stood up, grabbed Bobbi by both of her arms and walked her backwards, away from Monica.

"Look, Bobbi. You need to leave…this is not working. I need to figure this out and I can't do that with you here." He let her arms go and shook his head. "I still can't believe the mess you made here."

Once again, Bobbi was dumb founded by Savon's treatment of her. Not only had he asked her to leave while Monica stayed, but it sounded like he was blaming everything on her.

"So you're saying this is my fault?"

Savon exhaled. “Just leave, Bobbi.”

“Fuck you, Savon,” she said in a low deliberate tone. Bobbi was furious. With tears in her eyes she grabbed her bags, glared at them both and walked out.

Chapter 43

Savon made sure Monica was okay then followed Bobbi downstairs to let her out of the garage. And good thing he did because she was already backing her car out of the parking space when he pressed the button for the door to go up.

He could tell she was pissed off, but that was the least of his worries. Right now he had a dazed Monica sitting upstairs with what looked like a broken nose. Savon inhaled deeply and fell back against the door jam as Bobbi pulled off. It was bad enough that Monica's nose was probably broken, but he didn't think that would be half as devastating as the black eye he was almost sure she would have by tomorrow morning. After all, her face was her money maker.

How had his wonderful start to the New Year ended like this? Why did Monica think it was okay to just show up at his place without letting him know she was coming? And most importantly, why had Bobbi hit Monica so hard that he needed to take her to the E-R. Now everyone would be looking at him as if he was a woman beater.

He closed the garage door and went back upstairs. Bobbi, the publicist, had put him in another "spotlight" situation and he didn't appreciate it. The false accusation of paternity had been enough attention for him; now this. All he wanted to do was play football and live a quiet life free from drama.

He didn't see Monica when he walked back into the bedroom so he called out to her. She answered from the bathroom in a trembling voice. She stood there in the mirror looking at the indent in the left side of her nose. When she touched it, she broke down. She couldn't believe she had been punched in the face. Savon consoled her in his arms. He told her he was sorry for what happened and that he would take care of her. She didn't respond—just sunk deeper into his embrace. After awhile, he reached for some tissues and wiped her eyes.

"I need to take you to the emergency room for your nose," he said softly.

"I know." She sniffled and stepped out of his arms to look in the mirror again.

"Get yourself together while I get dressed so we can get out of here."

She nodded. "Okay." Her voice was low and shaky.

Leaving the bathroom, Savon closed the door behind him to give Monica privacy to clean herself up before they left. *Boy, boy, boy—this is a mess*, he thought. He grabbed a pair a jeans and a sweater from the closet and waited for Monica. He started to call Bobbi while he waited but decided against it. In reality, it was her fault that he was even in this situation. Later for her.

Bobbi wished Savon had been standing between the rear bumper of her car and the garage door so she could have run him the fuck over. That joker had some nerve making it seem like the whole episode was her fault. A person could only take so much disrespect; and once Monica pointed that boney finger in her face—that did it. Actually, she didn't even realize she had punched Monica until she saw her drop to the floor.

At this point Bobbi was so mad she could spit venom. Matter of fact, she didn't even know where she was driving right now.

After she burned rubbed out of Savon's driveway, she lost all focus. So she pulled off the road to gain her bearings. Once she realized where she was, her next thought was getting to Nikki's house to talk things out before she exploded.

Nikki was surprised to see Bobbi when she checked the peep hole. She opened the door.

"What's up, B? Why didn't you tell me you were coming over?" Nikki stepped aside to let her in and watched as Bobbi brushed past her—no greeting at all—looking like she was about to blow a gasket.

"What's wrong?" Nikki's words were full of concern. She hadn't seen Bobbi this upset before.

Bobbi looked at Nikki and sat on the sofa. She propped her elbows up on her knees and dropped her face into her hands. Nikki didn't know what was going on so she really didn't know what to do. The first question she asked Bobbi was if everything was okay at home with her mom and the family. Bobbi said yes. Whew—thank God for that, she thought. Once she confirmed that everything was okay at the firm, she took a seat next to Bobbi on the sofa.

Nikki rubbed Bobbi's back. "It's okay, sweetie." She wished she knew what had her God sister so upset. That's when she moved one of Bobbi's hands from her face and saw the tears. "Oh, Bobbi," she said with deep concern, "what's wrong?"

Bobbi couldn't hold back the pain any longer. She fell into Nikki's bosom and wept like her heart was broken in a thousands pieces. Nikki held her like she was a small child. Hurt and pain were evident in her cry but if it wasn't about a family member or her business, Nikki couldn't figure out what or who was the blame. Then, like money in the bank, her thoughts immediately went to Savon.

She knew Bobbi had been seeing Savon on a fairly regular basis, and that her feelings were growing for him so that had to be it. Her wheels started turning as she rocked Bobbi in her arms until the sobs calmed to an occasional sniffle. She didn't know what happened but what she did know is that it had to be pretty heavy for Bobbi to respond like this.

Bobbi excused herself and went to the bathroom. She needed that cry like she needed air. It hurt so bad to have Savon turn on her like he did after she had convinced herself that she could trust him with her heart. She exhaled deeply. *Punk ass*, she thought. She rolled off some tissue, blew her nose and cleaned her face then went back in the living room to tell Nikki everything that happened. She started with last night, New Year's Eve, when Savon told her that he wanted them to be exclusive.

Chapter 44

Bobbi didn't leave Nikki's house until five that evening. But before she left, Nikki made her promise that she would go to church with her tomorrow no matter how she felt, or how bad her eyes were swollen from crying. Nikki had someone she wanted Bobbi to meet.

On the ride home her thoughts automatically went back to the scene at Savon's house. Although she didn't regret tagging Monica's big head, the way Savon treated her really hurt. How could he blame her? Hours before Monica showed up, the light in Savon's eyes spoke volume for his feelings about her. She realized that he hadn't said he loved her, but he treated her like he did, and that was enough for Bobbi—at least for now. Had that changed? She had to know, so she would call him later, once she was settled in at home.

Nikki called to check on Bobbi around eight thirty that night even though Bobbi had called to let her know she made it home safely. Bobbi knew Nikki was concerned about her, and she would be the same way if things were reversed. They only talked long enough for Nikki to remind her that she would be over to pick her up at ten in the morning for church. It meant the world to Bobbi to have her best friend's unconditional support right now.

When Bobbi hung up with Nikki, she looked at the phone wondering if it was wise to call Savon. So far, she had managed to be tear-free for the last couple of hours and she didn't want him to say anything to upset her again. But how would she know what was up with the two of them if she didn't call?

Curiosity won over sensibility and she dialed his cell phone. Savon was still sitting in the hospital waiting room when Bobbi's number showed on his caller-id. He didn't feel like dealing with her right now, but he figured avoiding this conversation might lead to her showing up at his place later so he answered.

"Hello," he blurted.

"Hey," Bobbi said above a whisper; unsure of just how she should feel.

"What's up?" He needed her to state her case so he could be finished with the conversation.

"Uh, I wanted to talk about what happened earlier. I feel like you blame me for all the drama that happened."

Savon sighed. "Look, Bobbi. I know Monica showed up unannounced but you took things to another level when you hit her. Just so you know…she's recovering from surgery right now. You broke her nose." Savon tried to temper his words but he was getting worked up just thinking about the position Bobbi had put him in. "Now I'm sitting up here in the hospital looking like a woman beater or something. Man!" Savon rubbed the back of his neck and grunted.

Bobbi flipped. "Unbelievable. Whether you want to face it or not, this is all your fault; since you want to place blame. If you had handled your business properly, Monica would have never thought it was okay to just show up at your place seven hundred miles away." Her voice crescendoed. "Yeah, your shit is real raggedy. Obviously, you didn't end your business with her in a way that made it clear that the relationship was over. So now you have to deal with the consequences of your inadequate, ineffective ability to express yourself." Bobbi was ready to fight his ass now.

"Let's see if I can express myself clearly to you. It's over!"

Savon hung up the phone ready to explode. He got up and paced the floor. Another family sitting in the waiting room whispered about him to each other. The air became too thick for him to breath. He needed fresh air. So he took the elevator to the ground floor and went for a walk.

Bobbi had some nerve talking to him that way. Since they had arrived at the emergency room, the staff as well as others in the waiting area had looked upside his head like he was some type of sick abuser. And he was mad about it. He had even been questioned by police after they questioned Monica. If Monica had wanted to get back at him for being with Bobbi, she could have lied to the police and he would be in jail right now. But she didn't, and he was grateful to her for that. So as long as she needed him to take care of her until she healed, he would. And as far as Bobbi was concerned, she could lose his number.

Bobbi slammed the phone down and screamed. Once again, she couldn't believe how Savon was treating her. Yes, she had said some pretty mean things to him, but that was a direct result of him driving another dagger into her heart with all the talk about it being her fault. *Fuck Savon!* She turned off all the lights, fell across the bed and cried herself to sleep.

Chapter 45

At eight o'clock Sunday morning, Nikki stood knocking on Bobbi's front door. Bobbi had just come out of the bathroom when she heard the door. She pushed the curtain aside to look out her bedroom window and saw Nikki standing there with her hands on her hips looking back at her. Bobbi smiled at her and held up a finger to let her know that she would be right down.

"What took you so long to answer this damn door, girl. It's cold as I don't know what out here." Nikki stepped inside in her knee length camel colored wool coat and winter white boots. She rubbed her hands together as she walked to the kitchen. "Where's the coffee?"

Bobbi followed her. "I was in the bathroom. You didn't say you were coming this early." She started the coffeemaker. "I don't feel like going to church today. Look at my eyes. It looks like I went a few rounds in the ring and lost."

Nikki smiled and threw her coat on the seat next to her. Bobbi was right about her eyes. From the looks of it, she must have cried all night. But Nikki was determined to get Bobbi out the house today, so she would apply an entire tube of concealer to those bags if she had to.

"Don't worry about that—I'll do your makeup. All I need you to do is get showered and dressed so we can get out of here by nine thirty. Can you handle that?"

Bobbi rolled her eyes upward. “Okay, okay.” As much as she didn’t feel like going, she didn’t want to listen to Nikki’s mouth. Besides, she didn’t have much fight left in her any way.

Bobbi poured them both a cup of coffee as they sat on stools at the island in the center of the kitchen. Nikki took over the conversation. She talked about her job, the family, their mutual friends—anything to keep the conversation upbeat and as far away from Bobbi’s troubles as possible.

Nikki checked her watch and realized they only had an hour before they needed to leave. So she took Bobbi’s mug from her hands and led her upstairs to get ready. Dragging behind like a little child who didn’t want to go to church, Bobbi was pouting. Nikki looked back at her when they were half way up the staircase and shook her head.

“Now you know you need to stop acting like that. You’ll feel so much better once we get out of this house.”

Bobbi sucked her teeth. “I said I was going.”

“Then act like it.” Nikki went in the bathroom, turned on the shower, pushed Bobbi inside and closed the door behind her. Once Bobbi was dressed in a black pants suit, Nikki applied her make-up and they were out the door. Bobbi’s eyes were still puffy but it was nothing her shades couldn’t hide.

Right before Nikki pulled into the church parking lot, she told Bobbi about Sister Ruth, a community outreach counselor who just happened to be a member of the church. She told her that she had arranged for her to talk with Sister Ruth after church. Bobbi didn’t receive Nikki’s attempt at intervention well at all. Matter of fact, she didn’t want any parts of the idea. But that didn’t surprise Nikki. That’s exactly why she had drove, and why she hadn’t mentioned it until now. Nikki parked the car and went on to tell Bobbi that she met Sister Ruth while she was a student at Howard. Sister Ruth held a weekly session at a nearby community center where she talked to young women about healthy relationships with men. That part seemed to pique Bobbi's curiosity.

It would be interesting to hear what Sister Ruth would have to say about men. She was pretty sure it wouldn't be anything she hadn't heard before, but what the heck. If nothing else, maybe she would get a good laugh.

"I'll let you know after church if I want to go through with the meeting," said Bobbi.

"Fair enough," Nikki replied smiling at her. They went inside.

Unexpectedly, Bobbi cried the entire church service, even through the sermon. Every time she thought her emotions were in check either the choir would sing, or an encouraging word was spoken causing tears to flow all over again.

By the time the service was over she didn't have the strength to tell Nikki no about meeting the Sister. She just followed her down stairs into one of five classrooms.

Sister Ruth was already there talking with someone so they stood near the door until she finished. Ruth was modestly dressed in a brown wool suit with brown heels, and wore a single strand of pearls around her neck. Her hair was pulled back in a tight bun at the nape of her neck which showed off her dangling tear drop pearl earrings. She appeared to be in her late forties; her smooth skin was the color of a brown paper bag. Although her make-up was barely visible, her full lips were stained in a deep burgundy color.

When the young lady Ruth was talking to left, she walked over to give both Nikki and Bobbi a warm motherly greeting. She hugged Bobbi just as genuinely as she did Nikki.

"So Bobbi, Nikki tells me that you're going through a rough period in a relationship. I'd like to talk with you about that if it's okay with you?"

"It's okay." Bobbi felt comfortable and weird all at once. Sister Ruth talked to her like she might have considered her mentally unstable or perhaps delicate in some way. But at the same time she had such a soothing tone to her voice, and an authentic presence, that it put her at ease.

"Let's go have a seat over here," Ruth said pointing and walking towards a table and chairs in the corner. But before she took her seat, she told Nikki to leave them alone—that she could come back for Bobbi in an hour.

Sister Ruth could tell that Bobbi's heart was in a fragile state because of how swollen her eyes were and the obvious sadness in them. She knew she couldn't move too fast or ask too much of her in this first meeting. Hopefully, she would gain Bobbi's confidence enough to meet with her again.

Bobbi didn't know what to expect. It didn't feel like they were going to talk about men at all. It was obvious that the spotlight was shining brightly on her and would be for the next hour.

"Tell me what happened this weekend that has Nikki so concerned about you young lady." Ruth smiled.

Bobbi took a deep breath wondering where she should start. She decided not to tell Sister Ruth about her promiscuous lifestyle because she didn't want to be judged, and as far as she was concerned it was irrelevant. What she did tell her was how she and Savon met and how as soon as he asked her to be in a monogamous relationship, his ex came back in town unexpectedly to get back with him.

She went on to tell Ruth how Monica showed up unannounced to his house and flipped out when she saw Bobbi. From there things escalated, and the next thing she knew she had punched Monica in the face.

"I see." Sister Ruth was quiet for a moment. When she noticed her silence was a bit awkward for Bobbi, she continued. "And what did Savon say and do after you punched his ex?"

Bobbi felt the tears form in her eyes. "He took her side. He basically put me out because I defended myself. Never mind the fact that she instigated the whole situation. All he seemed to be concerned about was Monica and her broken nose." She wiped at tears with the back of her hand.

Sister Ruth's eyes stretched wide. If she had heard correctly, the pretty lady sitting across from her had punched another woman in the face and broken her nose. She passed Bobbi some tissues.

"Okay, Bobbi." I would say that's more than enough to be upset about. So what do you think about how Savon treated you?"

"I hate the way he treated me." Bobbi's voice quivered.

Sister Ruth pushed back from the table and went around to the other side where Bobbi sat and embraced her. And for the umpteenth time that day Bobbi cried.

"There, there, Bobbi." She lifted Bobbi's chin to meet her eyes. "Now… If you're willing to work with me, to be transparent with me, I can help you find peace in the midst of all this confusion and hurt." She rubbed Bobbi's back. "I'm not saying that it will be easy. Old wounds from your past may resurface in the process in order for you to heal completely as you work through the pain. I'm also going to ask that you face yourself in a way you may never have before. In other words, I may need you to look at your thoughts, your secret feelings—the things you hold close that no one else knows about your pain but you. Are you willing to do that?"

Bobbi didn't know what was going on. Who was this lady? She was asking things of Bobbi that made her uncomfortable. Why did she need to look at herself that deeply? This whole thing was supposed to be about Savon building her up—treating her like the most precious thing in his life—then at a moments notice, or more like Monica throwing a fit, he dropped her like she never meant a thing to him.

"Yes. I'll try," Bobbi replied with a bit of hesitation.

Nikki wrapped on the door twice and walked in. Bobbi and Ruth turned towards the door. Nikki asked if Bobbi was ready to go. Sister Ruth looked at Bobbi and asked it she could stay a while longer and Bobbi agreed.

"If it is okay with Bobbi, I'll take her home when we finish," Sister Ruth said looking between the two ladies.

Nikki looked at Bobbi and they both nodded okay. Then Bobbi told Nikki that she would call her as soon as she got home. Nikki said goodbye and closed the door behind her.

Sister Ruth didn't waste any time digging into Bobbi's past. She asked Bobbi what her relationships with men were usually like before meeting Savon.

Bobbi told her that when she was in her late teens and early twenties every man she ever loved either took advantage of her or cheated on her. She said that she was always committed in her relationships and tried to do everything within her power to keep her man happy so he wouldn't be interested in another woman. But for some reason it seemed she was never enough. So by the time she turned twenty-five if she dealt with men at all, it was only for sex and only on her terms. She said that being emotionally detached had been the best decision she'd ever made regarding men. Her chosen lifestyle had worked just fine for her until she met Savon and allowed him to get too close.

"I'll never let anyone else get that close again." Bobbi dabbed at a lone tear. "And I mean that with everything in me."

"Let me ask you one more question," Ruth started. "As a child, was your father in your life?"

Sister Ruth had never met Bobbi, but her story was one she'd lived herself and heard a thousand times in her mentoring. The face and names of the women were different, but the brokenness was all the same.

"Not really. I saw him every now and then. Why?"

"Did you feel loved by him?"

"No," Bobbi said above a whisper.

"Think about this," Sister Ruth began. "When a young girl grows up feeling unloved and rejected by her father, that un-nurtured need for acceptance and unconditional love sets into motion a very self destructive behavior. And often times, sex becomes a tool of manipulation for her; especially when she uses sex to try and win a man's affections. She will sacrifice her body, her moral integrity, and in the worst cases her health, seeking the love that went unchecked by her father. And the heartbreak that follows each failed attempt to gain love, chips away at her self esteem and self worth until she has very little standards for men to meet before giving her self to them." Ruth leaned in closer to Bobbi. "Honey, if every relationship a woman has with a man amounts to nothing more than her opening her legs, what value could she possibly place on her own life?"

Bobbi was stunned. She had never really connected her relationships with men to the absence of her father. And at this point she really didn't know what she thought about the things Sister Ruth said. *Is she trying to say that I don't value my own life*, Bobbi wondered with a bit of attitude.

Ruth exhaled. "Well Bobbi, I think we've talked enough today." She pushed up out of her chair and walked around the table to get something out of her tote bag.

Thank God. My brain is fried. And I think you insulted me Miss Lady, Bobbi thought.

She handed Bobbi a pen and paper and asked her to right down her home address and phone number.

"I know it was a lot to take in, and I know you probably don't feel like most of it applies to you," Ruth said. "And that's understandable. But when you feel like crying about Savon or talking about our conversation today please give me a call. I'd love to talk more with you about your life. Here's my contact information." She handed Bobbi her business card.

"Thank you." Bobbi managed a smile. She looked at the picture of Ruth on the card then put it away in her purse. But she didn't have anything more to say.

Six hours after she was practically drug out of her house by Nikki, she was finally back at home completely drained. She called Nikki and left a message on her voicemail, took a shower and climbed into bed for a nap.

Chapter 46

Monday morning Bobbi decided she would work from home all week. She needed her space and time to get her emotions in check. So she called her assistant, Cierra, to let her know and to have her screen and forward calls to her home office telephone. Cierra made notes as Bobbi rattled off what she needed her to do. Before they hung up, Cierra told Bobbi that she would call and reschedule all of her appointments for the week and send her and e-mail with the updates.

"Thanks, Cierra," Bobbi said. She would take Cierra a nice surprise when she returned to work next week. She was dependable and a tremendous help around the office.

By mid-day, Bobbi gave up on trying to focus on her work. Images of Savon and Monica kept flooding her thoughts. She was so hurt by the things Savon had said to her. He had gone from wanting her to be his woman one minute to treating her like she had ruined his life the next. It just didn't make since. And to top it off, Sister Ruth had messed her head up with all that talk about her behavior with men being a result of her childhood issues with her father.

Huhhh! She needed a drink. Bobbi went downstairs and poured herself a glass of wine. She walked over to the kitchen window, opened the shade and stood there sipping her wine. The weather was gloomy just like her mood. She closed the shade and went back to her office to shut down for the day. She called Cierra back and told her not to forward any more calls, but to take messages and she would get them tomorrow. Then she called Nikki to see if she was free for dinner. Maybe getting out of the house to get her giggle on with her best friend was all the therapy she needed. Nikki answered on the third ring.

"What's up, B?" asked Nikki. She was glad to hear from Bobbi.

"Well that's not the professional way to answer a phone when you're at work," Bobbi replied.

"B, your name and number came up on the caller-id. What do you want me to do? Act like I don't know it's you?"

"Whatever, girl. Look... You want to do dinner tonight? I need to get out of this house?"

"Sure." Nikki covered the mouthpiece while she talked to a colleague who entered her office. "B, I have to go. Let's say I'll pick you up at six?"

"Okay. I'm working from home today so pick me up from here. Bye." Bobbi hung up.

Nikki was concerned about Bobbi. She hoped that talking with Sister Ruth had been helpful. Bobbi was asleep last night when she called her back to hear how things went, but hopefully they would have a chance to talk about it at dinner. She had faith that her friend was going to be ah-okay.

At the restaurant, Bobbi and Nikki talked about family stuff and sipped on Strawberry daiquiris, waiting for their Oriental chicken salads. Bobbi would eventually tell Nikki about her conversation with Sister Ruth, but not tonight. She didn't want to rehash that drama right now. All she wanted to do was relax, and for a few hours try to forget the turmoil simmering inside her.

Nikki told Bobbi that she was going home for the MLK Holiday weekend and invited her to come along. She also told her that Gavin had tickets for them both for the home field play-off game the weekend after MLK. Bobbi's only response was that she'd let her know about both things by the end of the week.

Bobbi sipped on her cocktail. For some reason she wasn't having the jovial time she thought she would. Nikki was trying really hard to get her to talk but she just wasn't in the mood.

"I'll be back. I'm going to the restroom," Bobbi said scooting out of the booth.

"Okay." Nikki looked up and frowned as Bobbi walked off. This wasn't her Bobbi. Nikki sighed heavily then took out her Blackberry to check her e-mail.

In the restroom Bobbi washed her hands and rubbed them dry under the blower. It was definitely a bad idea to come out tonight, she thought. Once her hands were dry she checked herself in the mirror. She smoothed her hand over her ponytail and turned to leave. When she reached for the door handle a rosy cheek little girl with sandy brown pigtails stumbled inside.

"Whoa," Bobbi said reaching out to stop the little one from falling. "Are you okay?"

The little girl's mother was right behind her. "Please excuse her, she ran off without me."

Bobbi smiled. "Oh, that's okay. I needed to slow down any way." She chuckled.

The mother smiled back and took her child into a stall. Bobbi left out, headed back to her table. She took only five steps before she stopped dead in her tracks. Tony was standing at the hostess booth and he wasn't alone.

The woman standing close to him was attractive. She had almond colored skin and shoulder length brown hair flipped up on the ends. She was dressed fashionably and seemed comfortable with Tony. It didn't appear to be a first date.

For a moment, Bobbi hesitated. Although she and Tony were never in a committed relationship, she hadn't actually seen him with someone else before. It felt as if a small dagger pierced her heart.

Bobbi looked over at the table where Nikki sat, then at the entrance where Tony and his date stood. In order for her to get back to her table she had to walk past the entrance. *Huhhh!* She guessed she wouldn't be childish and pretend that she didn't see him. After all, she was the one who stopped hanging out with him to spend more time with Savon. So she took a deep breath, smoothed out the front of her jeans and sweater, glad that she was dressed much better than she felt; put on her game face and pressed forward.

"Hi Tony." She touched his arm and smiled at him and his date.

"What's up, B?" he said, happy to see her. He gave her a quick hug and kissed her on the cheek before he introduced her to his date.

"Sasha, I'd like you to meet a very good friend of mine—Bobbi Farqua." Savon's attention was clearly on Sasha.

Was that all she was to Tony? A "good friend". She knew it was true but somehow his introduction minimized what they had shared for almost three years.

"Nice to meet you, Sasha." Bobbi extended her hand and genuinely smiled at her. It wasn't Sasha's fault she was feeling crazy about everything all of a sudden.

"It's nice to meet you too, Bobbi."

Bobbi touched Tony's arm again. "Well I'd better get back to my table. She pointed towards the right side of the restaurant. "It was good seeing you Tony."

"And a pleasure meeting you Sasha," said Bobbi.

Bobbi choked back tears on her way to the table. Tony had moved on too? What was it about her that men didn't think twice about leaving her? Sure, her relationship with Tony was based on sex but they shared so much more than that. For him to introduce her as his "good friend" really hurt her feelings.

"What's the matter, B?" Nikki frowned at the look on Bobbi's face.

"Nothing. I'm just being emotional. Did you see me talking to Tony over by the door?"

"Yeah. I saw y'all talking. Why?"

"I don't know..." she said defeated. Bobbi sat down and looked at her salad. "I lost my appetite. I'm ready to go. Can you take me home now?"

"You want to get your food to go?"

"Yeah, that's fine."

So Nikki called their server over and asked for to-go boxes for both of them.

Nikki saw Tony and his date walk into the restaurant while Bobbi was in the restroom. But it never occurred to her that Bobbi would get this emotional over seeing him with someone else though. Then again, maybe it wasn't about Tony but more about her already feeling rejected by Savon.

On the ride home Nikki turned up the music deciding to leave Bobbi to her thoughts instead of trying to make her talk. Bobbi closed her eyes and didn't open them again until Nikki said she was home. Nikki reached over and gave Bobbi a hug and told her that things would get better. She waited for Bobbi to get safely inside then pulled off.

Chapter 47

Weak or wimpy could never be used to describe Bobbi's character. However, after all the crying she'd done lately, she was having a hard time even convincing herself of that. She was starting to get on her own damn nerves.

Last night when Nikki dropped her off, she went straight to bed and cried herself to sleep. Now she stood in front of her bathroom mirror looking back at eyes that were practically swollen shut. She sniffled. Tears threatened to come again.

Her thoughts drifted to Sister Ruth and the things she'd said on Sunday. Honestly, many of her comments were disturbing. But the single most chilling remark for Bobbi was that she could possibly not love herself. That was insane! After all, she took great care of herself; took pride in her appearance, and held herself to a higher standard than the average person, both personally and professionally.

Nah. That couldn't be it. Sister Ruth had missed the mark on this one. It was definitely about these wack ass men who don't know what they want. Settled in her thoughts, Bobbi took a shower, put on a burgundy velour hooded sweat suit, and went to work in her home office.

Around lunchtime she remembered that she hadn't checked her mailbox in over a week. Riding an emotional roller coaster with Savon was the main reason she had forgotten about it. One day she wanted to love him and the next she wanted to crack his nuts.

So after she ate half a turkey sandwich and a bag of corn chips, she pulled on a pair of boot slippers and ran outside. The air was brisk. She zipped her jacket all the way up before she reached inside the mailbox.

"Burr," she said once she was back in the house.

She locked the door and went back to the kitchen to sort through the mail. There were a couple of bills, grocery store mailers, coupons for pizza delivery, and a letter from Sister Ruth. Bobbi put the bills in her bill basket on the counter, threw the other papers in the trash, and stared at the envelope from Ruth. She wondered what the relationship counselor could possibly have sent her. She opened the envelope and took the letter out—it was two pages. At first glance it looked like more of the Sunday counseling session. It read:

Dear Bobbi:

Love yourself.

I know reading those two words probably make you wonder who I think I am to say them to you. But the truth of the matter is many women confuse self preservation with self love. What I mean is that when you're use to being disappointed by men, you automatically kick into "survival mode" whenever you get hurt. Because you're already intimately familiar with the sting of rejection, you learn how to function and survive with a broken heart. But that's not healthy for you, or what God planned for your life.

You are a beautiful young woman. And clearly you take very good care of yourself on the outside. But how does your "inside" look? How do you feel when you lay your head on your pillow at night and it's just you and your thoughts? Are you content with giving yourself to men who only think of you when they want sex?

Forgive yourself.

As important as it is to forgive others who have hurt you, it's also imperative that you forgive yourself. Sometimes hurtful things happen to us, especially in childhood that holds us hostage. And often times we blame ourselves for them ever happening. We expect our parents to love us. Yet sometimes life deals us an unfortunate hand whereby our very own loved ones are incapable of loving us in a way that reaches our hearts. So Bobbi, if you don't digest anything else I've said, please receive these words: IT'S NOT YOUR FAULT. You were a child—completely unaccountable and totally innocent when you were wronged by your father, uncle, cousin, grandfather, stepfather, mother, whomever.

So starting today, earnestly search your heart for those things that have you in bondage. Forgive yourself and LET—IT—GO.

Acceptance.

This may prove to be the most challenging of the three things I've mentioned here in my letter. Because after forgiving yourself and others, it's paramount that you accept your past. And I mean all of it—the good, the bad, and the ugly. This way, you will be able to move forward without that old baggage wearing you down and influencing your future.

We can't change the things done to us in the past, nor can we change the mistakes we've made along the way. However, we can decide to move forward in the fullness that we are special in our own right, and worthy of real love. When you can, read 1 Corinthians 13:4-7. This is how God loves us, and it will teach you how to love yourself and others.

Bobbi, God loves you. You matter to Him—and it matters to Him that you're hurting. Pour your heart out to Him. He's waiting to hear from you...

Please call me whenever you want to talk.

I love you,
Sister Ruth
(703) 555-1515

Chapter 48

Tears stained the letter as Bobbi allowed Sister Ruth's words to saturate her thoughts. Of all the things she considered to be the cause of her past failed relationships with men, a lack of self love was never a thought. And she couldn't lie—it was a tough pill to swallow.

For the rest of the day, she focused on the content of the letter and nothing else. Right now she needed to yield her thoughts to this new theory and reflect over her life.

By night fall, Bobbi was overwhelmed. Her head was swimming. There were three things in her past that weighed heavily on her heart: her feelings about her father; being inappropriately touched by a family friend when she was a teenager; and literally being used as a sex toy by her first real boyfriend when she was in the military. How could she forgive and accept all of that? She needed to talk to Sister Ruth.

She eyed the clock on her nightstand wondering if nine o'clock was too late to call the insightful older woman. She picked up the receiver, dialed the first three numbers then placed it back in its cradle deciding she should wait until tomorrow. So back in the envelope the letter went. She placed it on the nightstand and went to the bathroom to take a nice hot bath. Just as she reached to turn on the water, the telephone rang. She rushed to the phone and checked the caller-id. The name read: Ruth Abernathy. Who is that, she wondered.

"Yes." Bobbi didn't waste anytime with pleasantries. She had things to do.

"Bobbi. Is that you dear?" Sister Ruth asked, unaffected.

"Sister Ruth, is that you? I didn't realize your last name was Abernathy." Bobbi was embarrassed. The letter was addressed from Sister Ruth. It didn't have her last name on it.

"No worries, hon." She moved on. "Did you get my letter?"

"Yes, I did. As a matter of fact I wanted to call you just a few minutes ago but I thought it was too late. I wanted to thank you—again.

"I probably should be in bed earlier," she chuckled "but I'm usually up until ten or ten thirty most nights." She changed the subject. "Do you want to talk about the letter now, or would you like to call me some other time to talk about it?"

"Now is fine." Bobbi had a few burning questions for the Sister any way. She was feeling a bit exposed after reading the letter, so what the heck. It was time to speak freely—raw and uncut. Because in a way, her sanity was on the line and Sister Ruth's opinions and perspective were slowly gaining her confidence.

"Sister Ruth, I'm not saying that I don't agree with or believe the things you've shared with me, but I have to be frank with you—I actually enjoy sex. And up until this fiasco with Savon, I've managed my romantic life without any problems. I make sure the men I deal with have a crystal clear understanding that all I want is sex—nothing more. So far, I haven't met a man who didn't jump at the opportunity to indulge me in any way I desired because of the emotion free arrangement I offered. And as for me, it eliminates the 'getting hurt' factor because I never let my emotions control me. Like I've said before, I'm having this crazy situation with Savon right now because I messed up and let him get to close. But that mistake will never happen again." Bobbi blew out a deep breath. "So why does my approach to dealing with men have to be deeper than what I just explained?"

"I appreciate you being more interested in honesty than pretending," Ruth said. "Based on what you've shared with me, I believe you are operating in survival mode. I've been there Bobbi. The things I've shared with you are not ideals or text book theories; I'm speaking to you from real life experience. I understand that it may not make sense or be what you want to hear, so the most I can ask of you is to think about the things I've said and written to you in my letter." She paused a moment. "We all want to be loved. And we all need love. But you've convinced yourself that love doesn't matter because you haven't been able to find it. You think you've eliminated the possibility of getting hurt by keeping your emotions in check. But in reality all you've done is exchanged love for pleasure. Empty Pleasures. I'm sure you enjoy the addictive feelings and sensations that a man arouses in your body in the heat of passion. But pleasure is fleeting, and once it's over and he doesn't respond to you in the way you want or need him to, you feel used. Yet that doesn't stop you. You keep seeking pleasure to fill the void or emptiness consuming your thoughts whenever you're alone. And you may not want to hear this right now either, but once you love yourself completely, you'll clearly see how much God loves you too."

Sister Ruth heard soft sniffles on the other end of the telephone. "Love yourself, Bobbi," she said firmly. "Your heart is broken and it's crying out for love. Once you nurture it and allow it to mend, you will see your interaction and relationships with men in a totally different light."

"Thank you," Bobbi managed to get out. "I have to go now. I'll talk to you later."

"Good night, sweetie. Please take care of yourself. I'll check on you soon. I love you. Oh, and don't forget to pray."

With tears rolling down her face, Bobbi put the receiver in the cradle. After a while she got herself together and took a long hot bath. Before she got in bed she knelt to pray:

Holy Father, I don't know what to do or what to think. Please help me understand what is going on with me. I desperately want the hurt I feel right now to stop. But I'm having a rough time figuring out just what to do. I need you. Amen. And oh...please bless Sister Ruth. Amen

Epilogue

Five Months Later

Monica was driving Savon crazy. After the incident with Bobbi and the surgery, she moved back in with him. Initially she cried almost every day, especially when she looked in the mirror. As Savon had expected, the area around her eyes were bruised and swollen pretty badly from the impact of Bobbi's fist. It took over three weeks for her face to heal. Bobbi had definitely knocked her lights out.

At first Monica was apologetic and humble for how she had behaved in the past, especially about the paternity case and her refusal to stay and work through the situation. She asked for her ring back, and even wanted Savon to ask her to marry him again. But when he didn't give the ring back or follow through with another proposal, she flipped out and the old Monica was back with a vengeance. All she wanted to talk about was Bobbi and how Savon had betrayed her.

The nagging was driving Savon to drink more than he ever had in his entire life. He stayed out late every night hoping that she would be asleep by the time he got home. Living with Monica had become unbearable. One thing he knew for sure—unequivocally; and that was he would never marry Monica.

Now he realized just how much Bobbi meant to him, and he

missed her terribly. All he wanted to do was get Monica the hell out of his house so he could figure out how to get Bobbi back.

Bobbi, Nikki and Gavin were hanging out at Indi Blu celebrating Nikki's new job. She was partnering with a seasoned attorney in a small Entertainment Law practice in Rockville, Maryland, a suburb of DC. This was a power move for the two best friends. Nikki and Bobbi were planning a tag-team approach to their businesses. Bobbi would refer her clients to Nikki's practice and likewise.

After football season was over, Nikki told Gavin about Bobbi's incident with Savon and how devastating it had been for her. She purposely waited to drop the news on him after the playoffs—after things had a chance to die down a bit. Nikki knew Gavin cared deeply for Bobbi, so she didn't know how he would react if he saw her sad and crying all the time. But her gut told her that Gavin would have been locked up and Savon would have been on life support if she had told him everything when it initially happened.

Nonetheless, as soon as Gavin heard what went down he went to check on Bobbi right away. He stayed with her a few nights a week for two months. With him Bobbi didn't have to put her guard up or do anything special. He would hold her all night if she needed him to and he never tried anything. All the same, there were nights Bobbi would have to stay awake until Gavin fell asleep to make sure he wasn't going after Savon. Maybe this was love.

Sister Ruth had become more than just a mentor to Bobbi; a friendship was blossoming. Five month's ago when Bobbi received that letter in the mail she didn't want to believe the words held any truth for her life. But the more she tried to draw conclusions for what happened with Savon and every other relationship in her past, nothing made sense. So a month later with a troubled heart, she turned back to the message in the letter: Love Yourself; Forgive Yourself; and Acceptance. She allowed the truth to take root in her spirit and in her heart. And whenever she felt confused and sad, Sister Ruth was only a phone call away. Now, she still hadn't decided just how men would fit into her life, but she could honestly say that her heart felt lighter—stronger. The broken places were slowly healing.

"Bobbi, why do you let Gavin hug all over you like that? It's disgusting." Nikki turned up her nose.

Gavin hadn't moved his arm from around Bobbi's shoulder since they all sat down twenty minutes ago. Gavin squeezed Bobbi closer to him.

"Stop hatin', Nikki." Bobbi said. She smiled at Gavin and blew him a kiss. He kissed her cheek.

Nikki rolled her eyes. "Anyway. So how are we going to– "

Bobbi's ringing Blackberry interrupted their conversation. The caller-id read: Unknown.

Bobbi frowned. "Hello."

"Ahh, Bobbi. This is Savon. Can we talk?"

Where Can I Find Love

Can I find love in building a new house?
Can I find love in buying a new car?
Can I find love in buying a new pair of shoes?
Can I find love on a new job?

Can I find love joining a new clique?
Can I find love in changing churches?
Can I find love on a street corner begging?
Can I find love sleeping under a bridge?

Finally, I came to myself:
I can find love daily within myself.

© Joyce Newsome Bates

From the Author

Dear Reader,

I hope you were entertained by Bobbi's story. As much as I enjoyed writing about the oh-so-familiar struggles many women face with men, love, and sex – there was a greater purpose.

If Bobbi's story is a reflection of your own in any way – like it was mine for many years – you don't have to live your life confused, discouraged, or broken hearted. Be encouraged that there truly is real peace for your heart and mind. His name is Jesus.

If you've tried everything else to numb the pain – talking to friends, buying things you don't need, sleeping with random men just to feel wanted – but hurt still clouds your today and tomorrow, why not try God? In our weakness His strength is perfected (see 2 Corinthians 12:9).

It's all Love!
Icen

Visit Icen on the Web:
www.icenonline.com
E-mail:Icenbookz@aol.com

Philmark Motor Co

SAJDA24C8B1LF24614

5511 Allentown Rd

#301899-8877

Silver JAGUAR XJ8 VDP

Printed in the United States
218616BV00001B/4/P

9 780615 287164